Compass of Shame

Francis J Glynn

Wanderer Press

ISBN 978-1-9161242-0-2

By the same author

Veneer of Manners
The Salt Farmer

For my daughters,

Eily and Sheena

With love

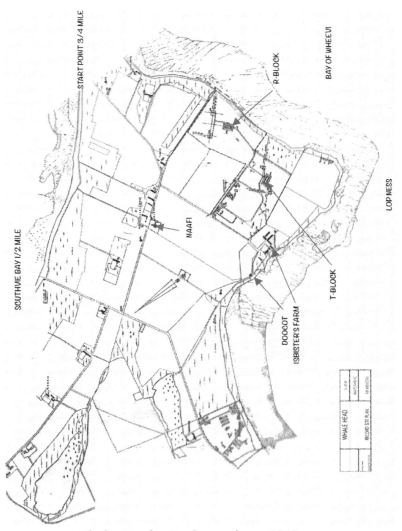

Whale Head, Sanday, circa 1942

PROLOGUE

sugar

The MV Hoy Head to Lyness, Hoy
Sunday 12th December 2010

The passenger lounge was warm, windowless. An old man perched uncomfortably in the corner, his shirt buttoned to the neck, holding on to a walking stick propped between his knees. A heavy-set man in a tracksuit moved to sit beside him.

"Good morning to you, sir."

The old man grumbled. The man in the tracksuit continued.

"Fine crossing today, is it not?"

The older man grunted.

"They say there's snow on the way."

The old man raised an eyebrow. The larger man stretched his legs in front of him.

"You're not from Hoy?"

The old man muttered under his breath and stared at the floor. The man in the tracksuit went to the drinks dispenser and poured two teas. He put sugar in one and returned. He handed one to the old man who took it, warming his hands on the cardboard cup. He sniffed at the steaming liquid.

"It's got sugar."

The man in the tracksuit took a sip from his own cup as the old man blew on his.

"How did you know I took sugar?"

The man in the tracksuit smirked. "I take pride in knowing about people, sir. By looking at someone, I can easily guess at their status in society, the state of their health, whether they have worries. By listening to them, I can tell where they are from. I can tell if they are trustworthy. I can tell if a man takes sugar in his tea."

The purser announced that they were passing The Barrel of Butter on the port side.

The man in the tracksuit grinned. "I've never been to Hoy. Do you know Hoy?"

"I spent time there during the war."

"You will have seen many changes then?"

The man nodded.

"Were you stationed there?"

"No, Sanday. They bombed it."

The ferry rose over a swell and settled.

"People died."

"I'm sure they did; and you are here?"

"So it would seem."

The old man grimaced as he moved, scratching under his collar.

The man in the tracksuit took repeated sips of the hot tea.

"Will you visit the cemetery?"

There was only the purr of the diesel engine and the sound of the sea splashing against the hull. The old man gestured for the younger man to come close.

"There was a girl…"

The man in the tracksuit moved around to face the older man.

"I was responsible for her death. And a man too, but he didn't matter."

"During the bombing?"

The man nodded.

"You were responsible? But the bombs were German, surely..."

Outside, unseen in the windowless cabin, seagulls called, hovering in the wake of the vessel. Wincing, the old man placed a gnarled hand over the younger man's. It was cold, covered in scar tissue.

The old man looked into his eyes.

"A terrible thing, a terrible thing."

The ship shuddered as it berthed.

CHAPTER ONE

$$Ag$$

$$Cd = S \qquad Zn = S$$

$$Cu$$

phosphors

RAF Whale Head, Sanday
Thursday 24th September 1942

Charlotte Hall peered at her screen. A wisp of smoke rose from the tip of her cigarette, adding to the surrounding haze.

"Unidentified target; range niner-fife miles."

She adjusted the gonio until the echo was a round, even pulse.

"Bearing one-three-fife degrees."

Charlotte savoured this strange vocabulary, designed to maximise comprehension. The information was relayed via the Filter Room at Kirkwall, to the Operations Room at Dollarbeg Castle, two hundred miles to the south. There, in the centre of the large hall, a plotter placed a token on the chart table, showing that the target was approaching Orkney from south-east.

Back on Sanday, at RAF Whale Head, in the concrete bunker that was R-Block, Charlotte flicked cigarette ash with one hand, scribbling calculations with the other.

"Approximate height, twenty thousand feet."

At Dollarbeg, a plotter added the information to the target token. The controller, overseeing the chart from a balcony, listened intently on his headset. He shone a little spotlight on the table, illuminating Charlotte's plot with a letter 'H'. The plotter raised her voice above the operational chatter.

"New raid appearing, hostile-one-eight. Number of aircraft not known."

The controller stood to view the chart table and reached for his transmit key:

"Scramble, scramble. Incoming hostile-one-eight at grid reference queen-edward-three-three-sixer-eight, bearing north-west, number of aircraft not known; approximate altitude twenty thousand feet."

There was a brief murmur from the plotters around the table.

"Blimey. The bandit's for Scapa."

Back in R-Block, Charlotte's heart thudded in her chest as the information was passed back to her. She focussed on the blip on her CRT. What had been a barely identifiable pimple in the shimmering green phosphor was stabilising, creeping from the right of her screen.

Outside, in the Isbisters' farm, pairs of pigeons hoo'ed together in a doocot, warming each other in the dimming Orkney day.

Fifty yards from Charlotte, in the other large concrete bunker, in T-block, telephone bells jangled. Sergeant Jack Cameron removed the pipe from his mouth and picked up the receiver.

"Hostile target identified, designated hostile-one-eight."

Cameron repeated the information, writing in his log. Across the transmitter room, Private Henry Long sucked at an unfiltered Woodbine, the rough tobacco smoke filling his lungs. He rested his head on the transmitter cabinet, feeling the vibration of the fans and pumps resonate through his body. Sergeant Cameron raised his voice to be heard over the noise.

"Private Long, can you confirm transmitter Standard Operating Conditions please? Hostile target detected."

Henry Long flinched at the grating sound of the officer's wheedling Canadian accent.

He remained expressionless as he extinguished his cigarette between thumb and forefinger, examining the meters and dials on the transmitter, recording them on his chart: anode current, grid voltage, HT. He calculated the transmitted power, copying the results on his clipboard.

In R-Block, Charlotte breathed in short gasps as she saw the target move across her CRT, the plot crossing the etched marker at sixty miles. She inhaled on her cigarette and relayed the new position.

In the Dollarbeg Operations Room, twelve young women moved around the chart table, squeezing together, their hands touching gently as they processed the information from the surrounding Chain Home RDF sites, simultaneously moving the tokens on the table surface. Above them hung a cloud of cigarette smoke and perfume that disguised the lingering body odour. On the balcony, the controller shone his little light on the token:

"New raid: hostile-one-eight, queen-edward-four-three-fife-eight, north-west, single Ju88, altitude twenty thousand feet."

An operator moved the German bomber's token to its new position. A flight of Hurricanes was now airborne from RAF Skeabrae as more RDF plots came in from the Chain Home stations.

The vein in Charlotte's neck throbbed as she listened to the confirmation. She too was thinking of the British Fleet, harboured thirty miles to the south. One bomber could be very lucky to penetrate the anti-aircraft batteries and barrage balloons that protected Scapa Flow. Then it hit her. The Junkers had not turned left towards Scapa Flow. He was heading on a direct bearing towards her own location, towards RAF Whale Head. Her realisation made sense; a Chain Home RDF station with minimal protection, a single ack-ack gun with no air cover for miles around. Charlotte tried to speak, but her mouth was dry. She sipped the cold tea, cleared her throat and spoke into her mike:

"Hostile-one-eight on direct heading towards this unit, repeat, towards Whale Head."

Charlotte changed her line of shoot. She identified a return signal that could only be the Hurricanes from Skeabrae. She did some quick calculations — they were on a direct intercept course. Outside the bunkers, the air-raid siren started its rising cry. Charlotte relayed the information to Dollarbeg:

"Friendly intercept targets detected at range four-seven miles, bearing one-niner-zero degrees."

On the chart table, an operator moved the token representing the flight of hurricanes half an inch.

In T-block, Henry Long observed Sergeant Jack Cameron writing the new information from R-Block. He drew in the bitterness from his cigarette, pushing the smoke from his mouth, exhaling a ring of vapour that floated out across into the space between them. It remained in the air for a moment before dissolving into the haze that filled the room. He spat away a piece of tobacco and walked around the transmitter, stroking the warm steel cabinet, peering into the little observation window where the valve flickered with a blue glow that bled out, lighting the smoky fug. The transmitter purred with the vibration of vacuum pump and fans, the gurgle of the water-cooled valve. The day before, Henry had replaced the control grid in the valve, the recorded readings up to the mark. Grid voltage was low, but the aerial current indicated that the massive pulses of energy, each lasting five hundredths of a millisecond, transmitted out into the ether. Forty miles away, the Ju88 reflected these radio pulses back to the receiving aerials, translated into the dancing green shapes on Charlotte's CRT. She passed on the new position; the Hurricanes closed on the bomber.

Charlotte selected a new line of shoot to confirm the position of the Junkers. She drummed her fingers as she waited for the image on her screen to return, for the new aerial configuration to engage. In that long wait, she watched the second hand of the clock on the wall stutter and stop; stutter, and stop. All she saw on her screen was the fading afterglow of the last plot. Her breaths shortened as she watched for the clutter to stabilise, but the image of the phosphor was fading. The clock continued its faltering circuit. Outside, the bomber was getting closer. She felt the beating of her heart pounding in her neck. She checked her settings once more; she called across to the telephone operator:

"Check transmitter status."

Across the receiver room, through the haze of tobacco smoke, the telephone operator relayed the message to T-block. Sergeant Cameron relayed the order to Henry.

"Re-confirm transmitter status please, Private Long? Expedite."

"Yes sir. What's the problem?"

"She can't change the line of shoot."

"It'll be the aerial selection relay. It's sticky. Tell her to repeat the operation."

Henry envisaged Charlotte on duty in the R-block, her manicured fingers stroking the controls, her lips close to the mouthpiece, the phosphor light reflected in her eyes. He scanned the indications on his transmitter that continued to emit its blue glow from the little inspection window.

"Transmitter fully serviceable."

Charlotte re-selected her line of shoot, waiting once more as the relays switched the signal to a different aerial configuration. As the screen came to life, she gasped as the CRT indicated the Junkers now ten miles away. She trembled as she comprehended the danger they were in, took a breath, reported their new position, while observing the growing returns from the Hurricanes closing on the bomber.

Outside the Whale Head transmitter and receiver bunkers, pigeons scattered from the Isbisters' doocot as the air-raid siren split the air; a dog stood, its tail between its legs, head sunk down into its shoulders. It looked up to the silhouette of the approaching bomber in the fading Orkney sky. The dog lifted its head, opened its teeth, and howled inaudibly against the rise and fall of the siren.

Charlotte observed the targets close on each other, knowing they were almost overhead. She adjusted the goniometer, her sweaty palm slipping on the Bakelite lever, and read out the position of the plot. In T-Block, Henry lit a new Woodbine with the embers of the last and squinted his eyes against the smoke dissolving in the haze.

Outside, the dog sniffed at something on the ground, barking at the incipient violence in the sky above. Charlotte's screen showed the plots of the Ju88 and the Hurricanes merge into a single blob that swamped the left side of her screen. She tried to relay the message back to Dollarbeg, her mouth now totally dry. She lifted the cold tea, put it down again, pressed the 'talk' button, and spoke into her mouthpiece.

"Friendly intercept in contact with Hostile Harry-One-Eight over this unit, repeat, in contact."

Above, in the darkening day, four Hurricanes flew at the Ju88, their gunfire rattling the frames of the fighters. The bomber responded with the thump of cannon fire. Below, Charlotte, unable to distinguish the targets on her CRT screen, wiped her hand on the rough material of the blue-grey uniform skirt. In T-Block, Henry sucked on his cigarette; outside, the dog darted for shelter, all the time continuing to bark at the bursts of light in the dim sky.

At Dollarbeg, the operators remained silent.

Henry glared at his sergeant beyond the cloud of tobacco smoke in the air between them. Jack Cameron glanced up, smiled and spoke in his soft Canadian accent.

"Nothing to do but wait, Private Long."

Henry clenched his teeth and grunted.

Inside T-Block and R-Block, Charlotte, Henry, and Jack Cameron imagined the aerial battle above them, unseen, outside their huge reinforced bunkers, when the building shuddered with the force of the explosion from a two hundred and fifty kilo German bomb; a few seconds later, another. Cups fell from desks, pens rolled to the floor. People stayed quiet; the lights shimmered briefly; transmitter fans dropped in pitch and recovered. Charlotte's screen went blank for a few seconds, showing only the phosphor afterglow. When the dancing green line returned, the shape of the pulse had changed. It was moving away, indicating plots of smaller targets; the characteristic pulse of the Junkers was gone.

Five hundred feet from the T and R-Blocks, a cloud of dust hung over two large craters. The pigeons returned to the doocot at the Isbisters' farm, the sheltering dog whimpered. Out past Scuthvie Bay, fragments of the German bomber fell into the sea.

Bay of Lopness, Sanday
Tuesday 14th December 2010, early morning

Jerzy Przybylski's eyes stung with the December wind that blew sand into his mouth, lodging it between his teeth. He spat, took a drink of water, and squinted, looking around, along the Bay of Lopness. He was comfortable with the rhythm on these islands. Close to the shore, was the remains of a First World War German Cruiser, its exposed boilers brushed by the incoming tide.

He walked further round to Tofts Ness, stopping for a while, looking out to North Ronaldsay. There, past the surf on the distant beaches, he noticed something moving at the shoreline. Through his binoculars, he saw sheep grazing on the beach. Light puffs of snow blew over the sea. Jerzy checked the map on his phone. Turning south, he continued across a farm track to the ruined buildings at Lopness, now used by the farmer as a barn. Nothing remained to indicate the function of the massive concrete structures; all that was left was the shell. Trees grew through the old transmitter rooms; the cracked concrete floor covered in moss. There was little to show of the vital work conducted here more than seventy years ago. Jerzy ducked into the small doorway. There was an aroma of damp, mixed with the smell of burnt candle-wax. Sheep droppings covered the floor. Jerzy saw something glint in the gloom, as he ducked to avoid the pigeons that flew out past his head. As his eyes got used to the dark, he saw a white shape. A body was neatly laid out on the ground, dressed in a shroud that reflected what light there was. Two burnt-out nightlights had been placed either side of the head; a box of matches on the ground. There was a familiar chemical smell in the air, and a discarded metal flask lay on the floor beside a crucifix. Jerzy crossed himself and smiled.

CHAPTER TWO

rare earths[1]

NAAFI, RAF Whale Head
Sunday 27th September 1942

"Don't sit under the apple tree,
With anyone else but me.
No, No, No."

The pristine harmonies of the Andrews Sisters floated across the NAAFI canteen from a Pye wireless radio. The warm damp air was thick with cigarette smoke and the smell of cooked cabbage, the room lit by the yellow glow from the ceiling lights along the semi-circular roof of the Nissen hut.

        Charlotte Hall placed her paperback on the table, face up, and delicately removed a cigarette from a crisp red and white packet. Through the haze, Henry Long gazed at her fluid movements, as if under water, slowly swimming, her long limbs like tendrils moving in space. With her left hand, she raised the Craven A to her mouth. From a gold-coloured lighter, a little plume of flame appeared. She held it to the end of the cigarette, which glowed to a crimson blossom. She inhaled, the haze permeating into her body, in some way making her contiguous with the air around her, making her the same substance as the surrounding ether. Squinting her eyes against the smoke, she removed the unfiltered cigarette from her mouth, and, with the same hand, took a piece of tobacco from her lips with her thumb and middle finger, and flicked it away. Charlotte lifted a mug of tea, sipped, then put it down again. As

---

[1] 'Earths' was the term used to describe various mined oxides and naturally occurring compounds of metals.

she smoothed the skirt of her RAF uniform, she replaced the cigarette between her lips, and, seeing Henry watching her, she paused. His heart raced as she smiled. He grinned back, but she had already returned to her book. It was as if she had not been smiling at Henry at all. He looked around, hoping nobody had noticed; he returned to his *Wireless World*.

Everyone at RAF Whale Head was shaken after the bombing. Outside, not five hundred feet from the concrete bunkers were the two craters where the Luftwaffe had missed. The Hurricanes had dispatched the Junkers to the bottom of the sea.

Like most remote stations in this war, RAF Whale Head offered few comforts. The accommodation comprised clusters of Nissen huts spread out over several acres; dormitories with basic facilities, one serving as an unheated cinema and makeshift church, and one large NAAFI canteen. The food was poor, but the farmers sold eggs, milk and cheese, the best thing about this posting, where the weather was unpredictable, and the prospect of a wet cold winter lay ahead. Cigarettes and tea were consumed in great quantities and constituted a currency of sorts, traded for favours and little debts. Sixty servicemen and women did three-month stints before returning to the island of Hoy for rest and recreation. Thousands of others had been posted to Hoy; servicemen and women from the south, who spoke like them and complained like them, about the weather and discomfort, many of them ignorant of the lives of the inhabitants who accommodated them in their midst. On Hoy, members of the Armed Forces had weekly ENSA performances: Gracie Fields sang for them and Yehudi Menuhin played the violin. They had the latest films and regular shows; and there were the dances, renowned and reported in the forces' newspaper, *The Orkney Blast*. For many, compared with Whale Head, Hoy was heaven.

But here, thirty miles north of Hoy, Henry Long lived with the wind and the hard, dark evenings and the misery that was his lot, with only technical manuals and back copies of *Wireless World* to read, and an endless supply of tea and cigarettes to keep him from losing his sanity.

He had no real awareness of it himself, but Henry was a lonely person. His father referred to him as a loner when he was a boy, and it had become a prophecy that had defined him as a young man. He avoided people whenever he could, but he was stuck in this miserable place: wet and windy, no let-up, the winter daylight limited to six hours a day, and no escape from other people. They all hated him; Henry could see it in their eyes. When he spoke, people didn't answer, and whenever he tried to do something decent, like holding a door open for someone, they would ignore him, without so much as a by your leave; not even a smile; so inconsiderate. He found people confusing and threatening, and he got by protecting himself from their bad manners. This had always been the way with Henry Long.

At Whale Head, there were two people who represented Henry's polarised view of humanity. There was Charlotte Hall, so beautiful but so unattainable in her immaculate uniform, with her wispy blonde hair and translucent skin that looked like marble, that shone with a luminosity that had the effect of an aura, probably resulting from the poor light and the persistent haze of cigarette smoke that appeared to make her shine. Henry was quite aware of this but let himself believe that this luminescence was her being. The mystery of women confused Henry: so wonderful, so different. He often wondered how he would ever become acquainted with a woman, or even speak to one, never mind the transcendent being that was Charlotte Hall.

And then there was Sergeant Jack Cameron, his Canadian officer, who thought he knew everything. Henry's technical knowledge was so much greater than that of his superior, but he would keep his insight to himself. Henry saw through Cameron, how manipulative he was, how he positioned himself in a room and used that sickening smile and the ingratiating Canadian accent. He had tried to befriend Henry, but Henry was having none of it. Hell would freeze over before he would acknowledge Cameron's pathetic attempts at friendship.

In the meantime, Henry's proficiency in the field of radio theory increased day by day. He devoured the manuals and technical bulletins, signing them out of the secure document vault as they were issued. Reading these manuals, he was animated, soaking up the knowledge he was gaining about this fascinating new field, lucky to be born into such a world. It had been just seven years ago that they carried out the first radio direction-finding trials at Daventry, and now here he was, young Henry Long, working in one of the fifty brand new 'Chain Home' radio direction-finding stations, the magnificent sites that had spread out over the eastern side of Britain. Each had three three-hundred-and-fifty foot pylons strung with transmitting cables, and a hundred yards away a pair of receiver masts. Each set of masts had an associated bunker containing the transmitter and receiver equipment – T-Block and R-Block. T-Block was where Henry lived and breathed: this world a whirlwind of technical advancement with a purpose. They had created a wall of radio waves that filled the sky over the North Sea, protecting Britain from the Hun. Here and now in Britain, in this war, a young man such as Henry could be at the forefront of science. Not yet twenty, he had had a letter published in *Wireless World*, and he was working on an article about cathode rays. He had become convinced that cathode rays, the blue glow seen in the valves that filled his transmitter cabinets, was the same radiation that formed the aurora borealis he saw in the night sky. Here was the single advantage of living in Orkney. Here, on the clear nights with the Northern Lights above him, he could develop his ideas.

Ayre Mills Roundabout, Kirkwall
Tuesday 14th December 2010, 10.13 am

Inspector Roland Clett coasted his old Polo into the Ayre Filling Station, the blue fuel light flashing. Next to him, Christine Clett tutted.

"I don't know why you leave it until you're running on fumes, Roland. You'll run out some day."

Christine fiddled with the radio, trying to change the station.

"The state of this car..."

As he lifted the petrol nozzle and placed it in the filler, he rubbed at a raised patch of paintwork that fell away to reveal a scab of rust. In the passenger seat Christine mumbled to herself as she rummaged in her bag, removing and replacing various items. She found Radio 2 on the dial and hummed along to an old Mamas and Papas song. She wound down the driver's window and called to her husband, who was watching the cost of the petrol increment as it entered the tank.

"Why don't you get yourself a decent car? It's not as if you can't afford one. You just hate spending money; you mean old bugger."

The nozzle clicked in his hand as the sensor detected the full tank. Clett gently squeezed more petrol until he could see it brimming at the filler, the smell of the vapour nipping his nostrils.

"Christine, I forgot my credit card, can you pay?"

Christine went into the kiosk, and Clett sat in the driver's seat. He winced at the music and tuned the radio back to Radio 4. Somebody was speaking about EU farming subsidies. His old Nokia buzzed.

"Good morning, Inspector. It's Norman Clouston."

Clett wondered why Clouston always identified himself so. His voice was as familiar as that of Clett's own wife.

"We have a report of a body on Sanday, out at the Lopness

Farm, near Start Point."

"Ok. Any other information?"

"Found by a Polish tourist; there's no sign of violence."

"And why are we interested?"

"The body is unusual. It was carefully positioned, almost ritual."

"Alright. Is Special Constable Tam Easson available?"

"Aye, he is securing the site and has talked to this Polish chap who discovered the body."

Christine returned to the car, settled into the passenger seat, put her purse in her handbag, and turned off the murmuring radio. Clett covered the mouthpiece of the phone and mouthed 'ta', pursing his lips into a kiss. Christine did the same. He continued talking into the phone.

"Norman, I'll be along to the station in five minutes."

Christine tossed her handbag on the back seat.

"Sorry Christine, I've got to get to work. Can I get you to you drop me off at Burgh Road?"

"You mean I have to drive this old thing back to Finstown?"

* * *

The first signs of snow were in the air. Out over the Peedie Sea, flakes fell on the water. They turned from white to grey and disappeared.

"You have an early flight tomorrow for Patrick Tenant's Trial in Edinburgh, and Geraldine Work's assault case is next week."

Christine squeezed Roland's hand.

"Don't overdo it."

Eddies of snowflakes whirled around the car and across the car park.

"I'll think about that later."

Clett reflected on two court cases. The first was the judgement following the trial of Patrick Tenant for the murder of student Dominic Byrd, in an archaeological dig on Westray in April. This was an untidy case with some loose ends that left Clett dissatisfied. Yes, the murderer was undoubtedly Patrick Tenant, he had admitted to it; but there were other issues that had been unaddressed. There was the actual role of the dig team leader, Trevor de Vries, who had committed suicide while in custody. Had he been involved in the murder? He had withheld information during the investigation. What was his past, and what did he do while running archaeological tours in Mexico before he came to Orkney? And there was the role of Ronnie Rust, the local nightclub owner whom everyone thought so much of – a man Clett knew to be a sociopath and drug dealer.

But it was the second case that kept Clett awake at nights; the brutal assault by the same Ronnie Rust on Geraldine Work, a fragile young local woman. An apparently straightforward case, but his friend Sigurd Rostung, the Procurator Fiscal, was now telling Clett there were problems. Rust had a history of convincing people he was somehow a force for good in the community, and he was now pursuing a career in local politics.

The snow was becoming heavier and Clett looked to the black clouds. In places, where the snowfall left merely a dusting on the ground, Clett was reminded of the scenes, just eight months ago, when the deposit on the stones was the grey deposit from the eruption of Eyjafjallajökull, Iceland. The massive eruption had grounded aircraft, disrupted ferry timetables and created uncertainty all over Northern Europe. The memory sharpened his recollection of the events surrounding the violent and senseless murder on Westray, of the student, Dominic Byrd. He entered the warm station foyer and shivered, passing the Christmas tree surrounded by Secret Santa presents. The desk sergeant nodded as he passed.

"What aboot this snow, sir. Think it'll lie?"

As he entered the large open plan office, Clett nodded to Constable Nancie Keldie typing at a computer screen decorated with tinsel and Christmas cards.

Crossing the office festooned with paper chains, Sergeant Norman Clouston muttered while chewing on a bacon roll. He pointed to a clean new file marked ORK/2010/12/14/Lopness. Clett lifted the file and went to his desk. He liked this unstable desk with its age-old graffiti. As he did every day, he folded a piece of paper to the correct thickness and placed it under the short leg. He ran his fingers over the old scores in the veneer. As he turned in his chair, it squeaked.

Clett moved some unopened Christmas cards, examined the file and considered the photos. The deceased appeared to be a man in his eighties, but nothing more was known about him. There were no signs of violence, and no visible signs of entry to the locus.

"Ok Norman, can you come in? Nancie, you too please."

The three officers squeezed around Clett's desk. Clouston was holding the remains of his bacon roll and a steaming mug of tea.

Nancie Keldie began. "We have a death in suspicious circumstances."

"Why is that, then?"

"The placing of the body is ritualistic. It appears to be formally laid out – these candles…"

Keldie moved some photographs.

"…and there's a peedie wee plate of bread nareaboots[2] that looks like a grey powder; placed there post-mortem? So, in the absence of a correct, ID, we've called him 'The Count', like Dracula, and all that, sir; you know?"

Clett rolled his eyes.

"I get the picture."

"Sir, somebody has interfered with the scene."

"Thanks, Nancie. Norman?"

"If this was not a murder, there are suspicious circumstances. Why go out to this remote site to die? A third party must have been involved."

"Igor, the Count's hunchback associate?"

Norman Clouston assumed a crouched posture:

"Yesss, Massterr."

There was a moment's silence, and they burst into a fit of laughter. Keldie dabbed at her eyes; Clett continued:

"As I was saying, we have made a preliminary approach to SPSA in Dundee. Do we need Forensic support?"

Clett looked at the computer images of the body. He couldn't get the image of 'The Count' out of his head.

"Norman, please contact Dundee with a formal request for support. I think we need a trip out to have a look. I'll get the next Sanday ferry and meet Tam Easson. Did he say anything else?"

"No. Just that he has established preliminary site protection measures and has taken a statement from the person who found the body…one Igor…no, sorry; seriously, his name is Mr Jerzy Przybylski."

"What else do we have? Norman. I believe you have results to report concerning your interest in the world of financial crime."

Nancie Keldie turned away to answer a desk phone that was

---

[2] nareaboots – nearby

ringing. She scribbled on a yellow stick-it pad. Clouston continued.

"Yes, sir. Have you seen that new cruiser in Kirkwall Bay?"

"That black monstrosity? At an angle, it kind of looks like a big black bird."

Norman Clouston coughed.

"It is the 'Vorona', Russian for 'crow'. The cruiser belongs to Oleg Komolovsky, a Russian Oligarch with an interest in Scottish investments. He has just bought a football club."

"Aye, I read about it; Falkirk Albion."

"Thank you, yes, they think he bought a struggling football club to launder money. I've been talking to the Civil Recovery Unit in Glasgow; I also think he might be involved in unusual currency transactions."

Nancie Keldie placed the yellow pad in front of Clett. He took a moment and read it.

"Well, Norman, that is very interesting, but can you put it on hold for a wee while?"

"What is it this time? Am I to interrogate some poor farmer for fiddling subsidies, or are we to fine a speeding teenage driver, or are we to get rid of a dead dog?"

Clett held up the yellow pad.

"Sergeant Clouston, this is Orkney and we don't have one of the lowest crime rates in the world for nothing. It is dealing with farmers and teenage drivers and dead dogs that is our world. I'm afraid that is the case, unless you are on to something big."

"You mean like counterfeit zlotys in Burray? Let me tell you sir, financial crime is real. It happens, and it happens right here, and under our very noses."

"Ok, I'm sorry Norman. We all know the success of your case of the counterfeit zlotys. Constable Keldie, this was before your time, but Sergeant Clouston really did discover a cottage industry right here in Orkney that manufactured currency worth 5 million euros..."

"7 million..."

"I stand corrected; that manufactured 7 million euros worth of zlotys in a bungalow in Burray."

Nancie grinned and then coughed.

"Sorry sir. I'm not joking, but we really have a code K9 DB. A dead dog, causing a traffic obstruction in Bridge Street."

When the sniggering died down, Clett addressed Clouston.

"Norman, sorry, but can you and Nancie deal with that? I need to interview this Polish chap..."

"Przybylski."

Clett looked at his phone. "Norman, Tam Easson will meet me off the Varagen at Sanday. Erik Skea is at the site."

The two men looked out to the snow dusting the fields around the Peedie Sea.

"Do you think it will lie?"

Norman Clouston tapped the window, but the tiny drift of snow remained caught in the frame.

"There was an astronomer called Przybylski who discovered a unique star in the sixties. Everyone thought it was made of iron, but he discovered it was constituted of rare earths."

"Rare earths?"

"You know, uranium, ytterbium, strontium, caesium."

"A star made of rare earths? Norman, what has that to do with – I mean, how do you..."

"You know, Inspector; books. By the way, Przybylski means 'He who has arrived'."

Outside the snow whirled in little vortices that danced across the Peedie Sea, like tiny tornados stroking the rippling surface.

* * *

Ronnie Rust took the large dictionary down from his shelf and let it fall open. He opened his notebook and wrote: Word of the day, 14th December 2010. He ran his finger down the page of the dictionary and found the word:

crepuscular *Relating to dusk; when the light is not bright.*

He copied the definition into his notebook and placed the dictionary back on the shelf.

* * *

As the MV Varagen rumbled out of Kirkwall Bay, Clett looked out at Oleg Komolovsky's cruiser. What on earth was a man like that doing in Orkney? He moved over to the warmth of the heated seat beside the grumbling coffee machine, next to a small artificial Christmas tree. He pushed back against the hard seat and took from his pocket a photocopy of one of Archibald Clett's letters. Clett had been compiling the letters of this seventeenth-century Orkney philosophe for some years. Like the others, this letter was overwritten first in one direction, turned through ninety degrees, and again diagonally across the page. The result was a tangle of handwriting. Clett could now read the letters with little effort.

> *To Mr Murdoch Mackenzie*
> *Kirkwall*
> *22nd April 1740*
> *Dear Sir,*
>
> *I write to you following our discussion at Mrs Eunson's coffee house in Kirkwall last evening. I fancy that we have the same worries about the safety of ships on our unreliable waters. You say that North Ronaldsay has seen twenty or thirty lost ships in the last thirty years. Such loss cannot offer prosperity for our islands – not to speak of the poor lost souls. The rousts and the ever-changing weather make for the greatest of demands on seafarers. Just last week, a poor ship was spent on Eynhallow. Thank the fates, its people were saved, but the cargo went to the bottom of the Sound.*
>
> *I can envision numerous light-towers on each headland that would be lit. A man would live there and keep it lit. I hear they have such light-towers in the rocky shores of the Mediterranean. Think on the great tower of Pharos.*
>
> *But this is a large undertaking and I get ahead of myself. I also like the little charts you have made of the Bay of Scapa. To have such a chart of the whole of our islands would be a boon to shipping. But we spoke of the organising of such a task. When I came home to my Mary, I engaged her in my cogitations on how to obtain the very large number of sightings that must be undertook to*

obtain the necessary accuracy. My good wife, so much more gifted than I in her perceptiveness, told me which you should instruct men in each parish to take such sightings. A single sighting, we agreed, was a simple undertaking. It is with the many repetitions that the multiplicity of data is collated. I would respectfully suggest that you supply each parish with a theodolite and show men how to use them. There are many such capable men in our parishes fit for such a task. I believe that you can supply a list of sites from which to take the sightings.

I am sure that others like myself could easily obtain a theodolite and assist in such a project. Let us meet at Mrs Eunson's establishment on Monday. I think I shall have the mutton.

Yrs.
Arch'd Clett of Canmore.

Over the tannoy the steward announced their approach to Loth, the ferry terminal on Sanday. Clett put the letter away and stood in the queue to disembark from the MV Varagen. Tam Easson was waiting on the quay. They approached and shook hands.

"Hello, Inspector."

"Hello, Tam. So, we're for Lopness?"

"Just short of the old Start Point Lighthouse. Twenty minutes."

Tam's SUV rolled along the smooth single-track road. The bruised sky above had grains of red, streaked through with dark grey, and it dominated the flat horizon. Here, there was so much more sky than earth. Out to the south, patches of rain and snow rolled over the sea.

"No snow here then, Tam?"

"They say it'll come."

"Over in Kirkwall, it looks like it might lie."

Tam drove east past the old German cruiser, its boilers all that could be seen, peeking over the surf. With the Bay of Lopness on their right, he turned right to an odd cluster of farm buildings made up of old crow-stepped gabled houses; an old abandoned doocot, shaped like a beehive about twenty feet high; some newer, more functional, harled buildings; and three large largely ruined Second World War structures that dominated the flat land.

Beyond, over the dunes, the Start Point lighthouse swung its beam through the flurries of snow out over the sea.

limestone

R-Block, RAF Whale Head
Sunday October 25th 1942

The Northern Lights lit the sky above RAF Whale Head, throwing shadows of the massive radio masts that blurred and shimmered across the wide expanse of the site. Inside R-Block, Charlotte Hall's eyes ached; her screen had been obscured by clutter that made it impossible to distinguish aircraft targets. She sat away from her operating position and blinked tightly. She had been staring at the green phosphor image for three hours. Any bump or blip on the line could have been a German bomber. She had zeroed the goniometer for the next girl waiting to take over the shift. The new girl was young, nineteen perhaps. Charlotte was only twenty herself but had fifteen months' experience as an operator – they only took girls up to the age of twenty-one. Where else could a young woman get such a responsible job, monitoring enemy bombers and fighters, passing on information that might mean life or death, or their own say-so, using their judgement and mental acuity? Charlotte and the other girls felt themselves lucky, thrilled to be alive at such a time. All the inconvenience, the discomfort, the rations and the indignities of the facilities in this remote place were as nothing when their role was so significant.

Charlotte handed over to the younger girl and went out into the cold night, out of the bombproof door and past the guard, a boy, about her own age.

"Watchword, Miss?"

"Stella Maris."

"Thank you, miss. Pass."

Charlotte was certain she saw the boy shiver. She gave him a smile and stepped into the open, under the starry canopy to the growl of the generator, to the soft singing of the vibrating wires strung between the transmitting masts. She took a cigarette, holding it in mid-air, unlit, breathing the chill air, screwing her eyes closed, still seeing the glow from the screen on the inside of her eyelids, the ever-present green line of clutter and targets that was the focus of her waking life. She opened her eyes and her vision slowly cleared to show the sight of the Milky Way smeared across the sky, tonight overlaid with the shimmering blue and green light. She was sure she still saw the CRT image on the back of her eyes; she blinked hard, but this light filled the whole canopy above her. As the wind dropped, the singing wires from the masts became silent. Everywhere she looked, the noiseless night was alive with a dancing curtain of light that emanated from a point in the sky directly overhead. It rotated, swinging its rays this way and that, shooting silent fingers of green and blue, with the odd splash of red-hue, from its apex high above her head, radiating darts of ionised plasma down to the earth.

Charlotte had seen the Northern Lights before, known as the Merry Dancers; something to do with sunspots and the ether. She had also known it had been the source of the high level of interference on her screen she had experienced over the last shift. But tonight, she stood in awe of the sight above her, not moving, holding her unlit cigarette away from her, unaware of the cold, unaware of her fatigue. The light from the aurora lit all the buildings and towers around. The transmitter pylons now crackled and glowed brightly, 'St Elmo's Fire' they called it. The blue light shimmered on the old Start Point lighthouse, now extinguished because of the war, but even its camouflage paint couldn't hide its bulk, silhouetted in the cosmic illumination that permeated all. Charlotte shivered and lit her cigarette, blowing smoke up into the chill sky, where it mixed with the blue green dancing plasma that streamed down from the ionosphere, vibrating with the wires.

Behind her, Charlotte heard the cooing of a hundred pairs of confused pigeons from the doocot, looking for light in the dim.

Lopness, Sanday
Tuesday 14th December 2010

Clett and Tam Easson left the parked SUV and crossed the field towards one of the huge concrete bunkers that now functioned as barns and stores for farm equipment. A tall man, his rucksack leaning against a limestone fence support covered in yellow lichen, was peering out to the north with a pair of binoculars.

"Good Morning."

"Good Morning to you, sir. What are you looking at?"

"I think I saw sheep grazing on the beach on that island. It is so far away. I am sure I am incorrect."

The man had an obvious Polish accent, but his English was good.

"Yes, there's a lot of that here. The sheep eat the seaweed. Makes for fine wool."

"Oh."

The two officers entered the old derelict bunker, ducking under the tape. It was a large space illuminated by the light that entered from a collapsed wall; a tractor parked at the far end. They exchanged pleasantries with Special Constable Erik Skea who was pulling a belligerent sheep from the crime scene. Irene and Sanja won't like that, thought Clett. He studied the body, which appeared to have been carefully laid out. The dead man had a weathered face, and wore a white, full-length shroud over a tunic, his fingers twisted with arthritis. Two burned-out nightlights had been placed either side of the man's head. On his chest was a saucer containing a dull white powder and crumbs of bread.

"Touch of the Hammer House of Horror here, Tam."

"Aye, sir; 'The Count'."

"So they've got to you too, Tam?"

"Sorry Inspector."

Clett bent and sniffed the body. "Ether."

"Yes Inspector, we got that."

"An Exit Bag?"

"Sir?"

"You know, a plastic bag over the head – suicide – with ether?"

"No sign, sir."

Clett leaned over the body and sniffed again.

"Definitely ether. Hmmm. No means of application, though."

Clett dabbed his finger in the bowl, rubbing the grey ash-coloured crystals between his fingers. It was gritty and dry on his fingertips. The white bread seemed fresh.

"What information do we have about him?"

"No ID; just 'The Count'."

Clett raised his eyebrows.

"Old burn marks on his face. Look at his hands: wracked with arthritis, but nothing obvious. We'll find out after the post-mortem; we'll have to see the medical records."

Clett sniffed again at the body.

"So: possible suicide, by inhalation of ether, but no indication of how it was carried out; no apparent means of application. Sanja and Irene will be here soon. They'll give us a clearer picture. Don't get this grey powder and the bread. Did he put it there himself, or was it put there by someone else? Too many questions. Where is the chap who found the body?"

"Igor? He's outside, Inspector."

"Igor?" Clett shook his head.

"Sorry sir. Jerzy."

They went out into the field full of sheep. Jerzy Przybylski was still scanning the horizon with his binoculars.

"Hello Tam."

"Hello Jerzy. Thanks for waiting. How are you finding this cold?"

"I am comfortable, thank you. It is colder in my Tatra foothills at home. But it is wet here. It gets to your bones."

"This is Inspector Clett, from Kirkwall."

"How do you do, Inspector Clett. I am Jerzy Przybylski."

"How do you do Mr Przybylski?"

The Pole performed a slight bow.

"Please call me Jerzy."

Clett found the man engaging. They shook hands.

"You are Polish?"

"Yes. I am on holiday."

"A bit out of season, isn't it? Jerzy, why are you here on Sanday?"

"I am touring around only. I just discover body."

"Did you touch the body? There is a small bowl with bread and a grey powder. We think they were placed there post mortem."

"No Inspector. I not interfere. I enter the room. I come out again. I find signal for my phone and report body."

"Do you know the identity of the deceased man?"

"I never see this man before."

"Thank you, Jerzy. We will have to ask you some more questions. Are you going to be in Kirkwall in the next few days?"

"Yes Inspector, I take ferry on Thursday. I go home for Christmas."

"Fine. Here is my card, please call me when you arrive on the Mainland."

"I not understand. You require to meet me in Scotland?"

Clett smiled.

"No, Jerzy, on Orkney, we refer to the Mainland as the main island here, where Kirkwall is. I would like you to contact me at Burgh Road Police station there."

"I see. Thank you, Inspector."

"In the meantime, could you please make a detailed statement to my colleague, Special Constable Easson. Leave your mobile number and do not leave Orkney."

"Absolutely Inspector."

* * *

Tam Easson drove Clett west and away from Lopness, the swinging arc of the Start Point Beam scanning the sky, filling with snow. They headed back to the ferry terminal at Loth. Light flurries blew across the road, lit by their headlights, the visibility to the south now obscured. Clett's phone buzzed as they picked up telephone reception, approaching the harbour. It was a voicemail from Kirkwall.

"Inspector, I've had a call from Inverness concerning the deceased Trevor de Vries, the guy who killed himself after the murder of that student on Westray a few months ago. It appears that significant financial data has come to light that you might be interested in. File's on your desk."

* * *

On Bridge Street, the traffic queuing around the block, the snow now blowing into corners, illuminated by each streetlight in a cone of white flakes, Norman Clouston and Nancie Keldie hauled the dead dog into the rear of the police van for disposal.

"This is disgusting."

"Welcome to the exciting life of the Northern Constabulary."

"Aye, the leading edge of the fight against crime."

Clouston's Airwave radio crackled.

"Romeo Sierra thirteen from Uniform Romeo."

"Shit!"

Clouston and Keldie repositioned the carcass. Clouston removed his surgical gloves, took the radio from its clip on his waist and pressed the transmit button.

"Go ahead, Uniform Romeo."

"Ah, are you currently involved in a task?"

Clouston rolled his eyes at Keldie.

"Affirmative Uniform Romeo, we are engaged in that code K9 DB."

Nancie Keldie frowned; there was a pause in transmission. The base operator then spoke.

"Ah, yes, 'disposal of a dead animal'."

"Yes, that would be correct, that is an accurate assessment of our current assignment. All for the good of Northern Constabulary and the community at large. Just what I joined up for, and it is bloody freezing, by the way!"

"Careful Sierra Thirteen, this is a recorded channel."

"Apologies Uniform Romeo."

"Ok, Romeo India seven has requested that you are reassigned. Can you return to base please?"

"What is it this time, are we to get a cat out of a tree?"

"No, Sierra Thirteen, India Seven said something about finding some money."

The dead dog reflected Clouston's smile in its dull eye.

"Understood Uniform Romeo. Returning ASAP."

* * *

Clett shook the snow from his shoes and placed his coat on the back of his chair.

"Ah Norman, thanks for getting here."

"Do I detect real police work in hand?"

"Perhaps. How far did you get looking through the finances of Trevor de Vries?"

"It's all in the report, Inspector."

"Come on, Norman. What else did you find out?"

"We didn't get very far. The funding for the investigation was pulled when Patrick Tenant confessed to the murder of Dominic Byrd. Why, all of a sudden, is this becoming interesting again?"

"Look at this report. It details movement of large sums of money between de Vries' account and a bank in Leon, in Mexico, the 'Institución de Banco del Banjío S.A'."

Clouston eyed the file, running his finger down the lists of figures. He whistled.

"In my investigations, I got as far back as 2006 at Norfolk University; open-ended transactions on his accounts for several tens of thousand pounds were identified. The money came in and went straight out again. Don't know where."

"Don't know?"

"Well, I, eh…"

"Please Norman."

"Actually, I can't honestly say. The international bank IDs referred to a bank in Mexico."

"This bank? The Banco del Banjío?"

"Yes, but I suppose that was to be expected. We knew he did archaeological tours there."

"Well, yes, but the number of transactions didn't match the tour group manifests, and these new figures are for such large sums of money. So, do we know where this money came from?"

"We'd need Chief Inspector McPhee's authorisation to get that information; I'm thinking of liaison with the Financial Crime Unit in Glasgow, maybe even the Interpol Financial Crimes Unit."

"Why didn't this happen at the time?"

"As I said, the case was closed; all budgeting was frozen when de Vries admitted the murder."

"We have to open it again. I'll fix the paperwork side. Let me know what signatures and authorisations are required. Find out about this money; find out where de Vries got the money. We need any links that can connect to Orkney, or Norway or to Dominic Byrd, or especially, dare I say it, to Ronnie Rust."

"Great. Leave it with me, I'll get on to it."

"Don't you want to get to the smell of dead dog off you first?"

"I'll just get cracking, if you don't mind."

"Much as it pains me to say it, I wonder if our friend DI Nelson may have been on to something."

"What, you mean that de Vries killed Byrd after all?"

"I wouldn't go as far as that, but this lead opens up the possibility of drug connections in Mexico. This case isn't over yet."

The muscles in Clett's neck were tight; solid. He rubbed, but it only became more painful. As he exhaled, there was a pounding in his whole head. His temples and eyes throbbed in a cruel sympathy. He called Christine.

"Can you pick me up? I have to get some sleep before the early flight to Edinburgh tomorrow."

"Sure, Roland. See you in fifteen minutes."

Clett looked out to the cones of whirling snow caught in the streetlights that swayed in the wind; the sole illumination in the darkening sky.

* * *

Ronnie Rust scanned the shelves in The Orcadian bookshop and found the 'Self Help' section. He ran his finger over the familiar titles until he found what he was looking for. The writing on the spine read 'Be Your Own Personal Guru' by Sri Swami Samananda. He had read the reviews and was about to remove the it from the shelf, when his eye was drawn to Gerauld Surrmann's new book, 'The Science of the Inner You'. He took the book, opened it and read a sentence at random:

Are you afraid of sex?

Rust's heart raced. He closed the book with a thump; he glanced around the bookshop, sweat forming on his brow. There was a tall, thin man looking at angling magazines; a young well-dressed woman caught his eye and stared. The woman behind the desk put her phone down and smiled at him. Rust returned the smile with uncharacteristic nervousness, hiding the book behind his back.

* * *

Sanja Dilpit and Irene Seath lifted their bags from the carousel and wheeled them across the terminal at Kirkwall airport.

"Ah think we were lucky tae land."

"Aye, they'll be closin' the airport for sure wi' a' this snow."

Irene caught her reflection in the mirror of a display cabinet.

"Checkin' yer mascara?"

"Naw. Ah think ah overdid it, pluckin' ma eyebrows."

"Tweezer happy?"

"Aye, mibbe."

"Never mind. At least they're straight."

"Ah dunno. Dae ye think so?"

"Come on. There's a taxi."

Byres Road, Glasgow
that evening

Sandy and Magnus Clett sipped their lagers; around them, Christmas office parties in full flow. The door opened and shut, bringing wafts of cold air from Byres Road. Magnus stared at Sandy; his eyes half shut.

"Are you tired? You don't look well."

He peered again at his brother's pale complexion in the dark bar. "Haven't taken anything, have you?"

"Eh; don't be daft, I'm just tired."

Sandy looked away.

"Life's good. The product has really taken off and we might be bought out by Envidiom; they're big in pattern recognition algorithms; but never mind that, I wanted just to catch up. Mainly to tell you that Jane and I are getting married."

Sandy looked up at Magnus and smiled for the first time in the conversation.

"That's great, Magnus. I didn't even know you were back together."

"Aye, I popped the question. She said yes."

"Brilliant news, Magnus. I'm very happy for you. Have you told Mum and Dad?"

"Not yet. I wanted you to be the first to know. We want you to be best man."

Sandy hugged his brother.

"Thanks Magnus, I'd love to. I appreciate this. I needed good news like this."

They separated. Sandy looked down at his feet.

"What's wrong, Sandy?"

"Nothing really."

"Come on Sandy, I can see you're not in good shape."

"I've been missing lectures. Don't know why. I just can't be bothered."

"But you love psychology. What about the hard work you did to get into the course? You loved the placement you did out at Drumchapel."

"Aye. I eh, I'm just tired of it all. It is all just...meaningless."

Magnus stared at his brother again. Sandy's shoulders were hunched; he seemed smaller that his full height of nearly six foot, his eyes a weary yellow. He affected a smile.

"But Magnus, tell me more about the wedding. Have you fixed a date?"

Sandy slowly lifted his pint to his mouth.

* * *

The silent birds fluttered in their sleepy nests, offering no reason to stay awake. Clett got into bed beside Christine. She was warm. He lay close and put his arms around her.

"Mmmmhhhh. You're cold."

She turned over to face him. He kept his stubbly cheek away from her.

"Roland, you know…"

"Yes, I know."

"I have work in the…"

"It's ok."

"I'm sorry."

"Don't worry about it."

"I'm…."

"Go to sleep."

Clett closed his eyes.

caffeine

NAAFI, RAF Whale Head
Thursday 12th November 1942

"Hello, folks, Jack Benny here. What a wonderful day. On a day like this, let me tell you: give me golf clubs, fresh air and a beautiful partner. On second thoughts, you can keep the clubs and the fresh air."

The studio audience roared in laughter. Charlotte Hall filed her nails and smiled. Benny's nasal tones emitted from the Pye wireless radio set in the corner of the NAAFI, tuned to the Forces Network. A swing band started up a manic foxtrot. Charlotte crossed her legs, her upper foot tapping rapidly in time with the music. She tore away the crisp foil from a new pack of Craven A. The scent of fresh tobacco filled her nostrils, promising that still sense at the first draw: 'Made specially to prevent sore throats!' It said so in the advertisements. She brought the perfect cigarette to her lips. Holding her lighter, she examined the engraving:

For Charlotte,
with all my love,
your Jim.

A tiny lick of flame emitted from the lighter. She applied it to the end of her cigarette, sucking in the smoke, blowing out through her nose, letting calm permeate her upper body. As she felt her shoulders relax, she practiced holding the cigarette away from her, at arm's length, the way she had seen Greta Garbo do in the movies. She twisted, examining the line of her eyebrow pencil on the back of her leg; from a respectable distance, it looked just like a stocking seam.

On the other side of the NAAFI, Henry struck a Vesta in a splash of sparks. The match-head flared, he lit his cigarette, jabbing the match, sucking until the end glowed an angry red. He drew in the acrid smoke, relishing the sharp sensation radiating through his chest. As he engaged in this little ritual, he watched Charlotte through the soft haze, pretending to read his *Wireless World*, his thoughts far from circuit diagrams and radio theory.

Henry yearned to touch Charlotte, to smell her, to stroke her shoulder, or her leg, or any part of her beautiful uniformed body. She had become the focus of his waking thoughts. He wrote down her duty hours and made sure he was around when she was off, when they worked the same hours, he listened to her voice on the r/t. He had found a way of patching her headset mike to an earpiece so he could hear her when she wasn't transmitting: her breathing, murmuring to herself, and to the drumming of her fingernails on the desk.

It took four days for Henry Long to see her as she was this afternoon, across the canteen, radiating everything that he desired. He had written a plan which he carried with him, so he could change and update at any time. He had created a matrix showing her work hours, and his; there were spaces marked as possible periods of time he could approach her. He had to be patient; but he was so desperate to touch her. He ached with desire for her. Across the room, he watched her as she stretched her long body and yawned. He loved it when she stretched. She lifted her arms over her head; as she did so, her skirt lifted an inch. Henry gazed at the patch of her beautifully tanned leg. She relaxed and saw him watching. She smiled that incredible smile; he smiled back nervously, and returned to his magazine, the words a blur. She had smiled at him; this time, there was no doubt about it. Now was the time; this was his moment. He placed the magazine on the table and closed his eyes, reciting to himself the words he had worked out. He took a deep breath.

"Hello Miss. Charlotte, isn't it?"

"Yes, I was hoping you would say hello. You're Henry, aren't you? Why don't you sit down?"

Henry imagined his fingers touching the fabric of her uniform at her elbow. He savoured her perfume in his mind. But when he opened his eyes from his reverie, she was still there, across the NAAFI tearoom, still filing her nails, her Craven A cigarette resting in an ashtray, its single thread of smoke rising into the NAAFI's little fog. She smiled again. Now, now, now. His heart was racing as he pushed his chair from the table, grating on the floor; but as he stood to approach her, Sergeant Jack Cameron opened the blast door and briskly entered, bringing a wave of cold air.

"Hi there, Private Long."

"Sir."

Henry sneered and affected a lazy salute. He put out his cigarette, squeezing its lit-end between his fingers, focussing on the sharp pain. He blew the ash from his scorched fingertips as he slumped back in the chair. Cameron poured himself a mug of tea from the urn.

"Ah, sugar today. Super."

Henry glared as Cameron poured fresh milk from a jug, and approached Charlotte, who was extinguishing a cigarette.

"Do you mind if I join you, Miss?"

"Not at all, Sergeant."

"Call me Jack," he said in his gentle Canadian drawl.

"How do you do? I'm Charlotte Hall."

"I recognise your voice from the r/t, but I think this is the first time we've met. I work in T-Block."

"But Sergeant, you shouldn't be telling me this. Walls have ears, and all that."

"Let's keep it between us, shall we?"

Henry observed over the top of his Wireless World as they shared their little pleasantries. Cameron offered a cigarette to Charlotte. Henry struggled to hear them over the wind rattling the windows and the sibilant sounds of the Forces Radio. The mad foxtrot had finished, and Jack Benny had returned, broadcasting that unmistakable mocking, nasal delivery, followed by loud audience laughter and harsh-sounding applause. Henry cupped his hand to his ear, trying to listen to snatches of their conversation.

"Have one of mine," said Cameron.

"Very kind of you. Are you American?"

"Canadian."

Cameron took a lighter from his pocket, flipped the top, and ignited the wick, holding the flame close to Charlotte's face. He pointed to the wings on his shoulder.

"Royal Canadian Air Force. I came from our RDF training establishment at Clinton, fifty miles north of London, Ontario. Your chaps needed our expertise. We were happy to oblige, you know, doing our bit for Blighty."

"We're glad you're here, Sergeant...Jack."

Coyly, Charlotte looked down, then lifted her cup, sipped, and frowned.

"I ruddy well hate cold tea."

Cameron smiled.

"Can I get you another?"

"Would you? Milk and two please."

"Ah yes, they have sugar today."

Grinning at Charlotte, who was still considering her nails, Cameron went to the urn and poured the thick dark liquid into a teacup. Across the tearoom, Henry took out his matrix, placing it over a circuit diagram. The next gap in their rota would be in three days; another three days before he could see Charlotte again. The music had stopped, Jack Benny was eliciting more laughter from his studio audience, their applause sinuously hissing from the speaker. Cameron returned to Charlotte, putting the cup of tea in front of her.

"How do you like Whale Head?"

"The Northern Lights are lovely."

"Long way from home?"

"And quiet."

"What about that flap last month – the Junkers?"

Charlotte whispered. "I found it, you know. Golly gosh! I shouldn't say, really, but it was just so thrilling."

Cameron nodded, looking around. No one was listening, only Private Henry Long at the opposite end of the tearoom.

"We shouldn't really speak about it though."

"Of course not, but do you know, I thought the kit was goosed for a minute."

"Sure. Known problem. Fixed now. Sticky relay."

"Relay? Really?"

They both smiled. Henry cursed himself as he saw Cameron rise to his feet.

"Must be off. There's a war to fight. Chin chin. Cheerio, Charlotte."

"Oh well. Cheerio Sergeant, em, Jack. I'll see you next time."

They shook hands, and Cameron left the NAAFI. Jack Benny was now saying something in his staccato articulation. The audience laughter subsided. Henry looked again at the matrix. He stood in a cold sweat. He moved a chair out of his way, his knees shaking as he walked across the floor. All he had to do was repeat his rehearsed little speech. She had a last sip of her tea and stood up to leave. They were eye to eye. Henry opened his mouth. Charlotte smiled and looked at him.

"Hello Henry."

At the sound of his name, under the power of her gaze, his focus evaporated, swirling in her perfume and her smile. He sweated, tried to speak. He was unable look her in the eye. The room swayed and rolled beneath his feet. The laughter from the radio overpowering, Henry was tongue tied and his nerves now controlled his every thumping heartbeat. He was mute, immobile; all his rehearsal, all his preparation for nothing. His jaw opened and closed, and he grunted.

"Eh, eh, I'm eh, I'm sorry."

"Are you alright Henry?"

He stepped back, bumping into a table. A chair clattered to the floor, and he bent to pick it up.

"Sorry Charl miss... I, eh..."

He reversed as far as the blast door, turned and ran out into the wind and rain. It was a rain that, although light, persisted. In a few moments, Henry was soaked through to his shirt and vest. He wanted the world to make him vapour; he wanted never to have existed. What kind of a man was he that he dissolved at the smile of a woman? He felt no cold, only shame, shame, shame. What cruel force was it that put him into this world, so ugly, so repulsive; such a creature that he could never ever communicate with a woman. But along with his disgust and self-hatred, came a realisation; Henry would never again humiliate himself in such a fashion. Never. But he also knew that it was really not enough. His shame was turning to anger. There had to be something he could do to prove his worth. What could he do to claim his space on this earth?

High Court, Edinburgh
Wednesday 15th December 2010

The High Street was coated in a thick layer of snow that lay pristine on the roofs, depositing delicate brushstrokes on each little historic feature. The road had been salted the night before; the dirty spray from the buses and cars had created piles of brown slush at the edge of the kerbs. Little patches had become compressed and icy, and people were corralled into the centre of the pavements, their shoulders touching uncomfortably as they passed each other.

The heavy snow fell still, and the traffic was hushed. The sounds of the crowd slowed to a murmur. Clett walked out of the High Court into the silent Christmas throng. He called Chief Inspector Maggie McPhee, the senior officer at Kirkwall Police Headquarters.

"You must be happy to draw a line under all this, Roland."

"Happy? No, Maggie, not happy."

"Of course; not happy. I see that."

The Christmas shoppers squeezed together in the bottleneck at the huge statue of David Hume. At head height, passers-by would touch his big toe, so its patina was lost, exposing the shiny brass beneath.

"What was the deliberation, Roland?"

"Twelve years. The poor man made quite the pathetic case in the dock; his wife was in tears during the whole thing."

Clett had seen this spectacle before. An ordinary person, placed in an extraordinary situation, acting thoughtlessly, causing the utterly needless death of another human being. There was no viciousness here. Clett had known killers but never met one who was crazed or manipulative. People bewildered by their actions, who could not understand what had brought them to this end. In other respects, no different from anyone else other than the knowledge that they had done that thing that made them apart.

"And you're back here for Ronnie Rust's assault case next week; and all before Christmas. Please take it easy, Roland. Try to pace yourself."

Clett looked at the snow-covered tree in front of St Giles. A gift from the Norwegian people for the support given by the people of Scotland during the Second World War. Another component in the multiple interweaving narratives that melded together to make up the Christmas story. Which of these Christmas shoppers gave it a thought?

"I'll be on the next flight back to Orkney."

Clett reached up and touched David Hume's cold, shiny brass toe.

* * *

Back on Sanday, dressed in white disposable overalls, Sanja Dilpit and Irene Seath were recording information at the workspace adjacent to the body. Irene was dusting a metal flask they had found about fifty feet away.

"Still smells of ether."

"Inspector Clett thinks it was an exit kit."

"Ok, but he still needs a hanky, or a plastic bag, or something that he can use to contain the ether for it to be ingested."

"Might be anywhere; maybe blown away by now."

Sanja was crouched over the body. "Jesus! Come quick."

Irene dashed to where Sanja was crouched over the body.

"Look there. Can ye see?"

"Whit?"

"Puncture marks on his throat."

"Where?"

"There. Definitely fang marks."

The two burst out laughing.

"Christ, ye got me there, hen."

The laughter died down and they returned to their work.

"So, still no ID?"

"Just 'The Count'."

"Aye, Ah know," Irene grinned. "Ah've sent aff the prints, and DNA. If there's a pair of incipient fangs in the dentals, we've got our man."

Sanja rolled her eyes. "Come on, hen. Stick wi' the script. We need to see what was on his computer."

Irene bent over the body placed a finger into the grey powder. Gingerly, she sniffed it, and held it up to the light. She placed some on a slide and examined it under a microscope. She then removed her glove and rubbed the substance between thumb and forefinger. She dabbed it on her tongue.

"It's salt."

"No way!"

"It is. No like rock salt, or sea salt, or refined salt, but it is salt. I read about these mines in Columbia that produce this primitive salt. The colouration is from sandstone and other minerals. Ye cannae buy this in Tesco."

"Good girl. Whit about the bread?"

"We might be able to date that bread; see when it was bought."

"Aye, an' I'll get the salt sent for spectrum analysis. Let's see if we can find where it came from."

"An' there's some fragments of fingerprints on the edge of the bowl, but not enough for a match."

They returned to the body and turned it over. Beneath the shroud, the dead man was wearing a thick tunic made of animal skin with the hairs on the inside.

"Jeez. What's he's wearing?"

Finstown, Orkney
Thursday 16th December 2010

Clett looked out of his study window to the garden below, the old rowan half covered in snow. It had three intertwined trunks, wrapped around the large rocks placed there by him and Magnus and Sandy when they were small. The stones were now locked in this woody embrace, subject to the constant rain and intermittent sunshine that nourished them. Clett had two photocopies in his hands as Christine came up the stairs.

"Thought you might..."

Clett cleared an area of the desk and Christine put the cup of tea down. He put his arm around her waist and she moved closer to him as a cloud cleared and the late morning sun warmed them. They were silent for a moment and then she rubbed his bald head and bent down to kiss it.

"How's old Archibald Clett doing?" she asked.

"Oh, coming along. Every time I think I'm making progress; I find more work to do."

"As long as you're not being too distracted by Ronnie Rust's court case."

A pair of wood pigeons perched together in the rowan, sheltering from the blowing snow.

"*Lesnoy golub.*"

"Sorry?"

"Wood pigeon – Russian."

"Hmm. You never followed up on your Russian. Don't you miss it?" Clett took up one of the sheets of paper. He examined the photocopied letter.

> *To Mr Murdoch Mackenzie*
> *Kirkwall*
> *October 15th 1746*
> *Dear Sir,*
> *Further to our conversations concerning the production of charts for the safety of our ships, We agree that in order to create charts of the seas, we first have to create charts of the lands that are bounded by these seas. In order to do this, you say to me we have to create a little meridien. A datum from which we expand, creating more datums, each fixed in accuracy by the repeated recordings of sightings, each repetition increasing the reliance of the next datum to be measured. But first, we require our prime meridien – You have suggested that we need a fixed chain of a known, precise length, and to run it along a piece of land with no variations in height. A piece of land with no striation or variation in height? Where are we to find such a site upon our Orkney?*
> *Yrs, &c.*
> *Arch'd Clett of Canmore*

Clett typed some corrections to the transcription. Outside, the snow blew in flurries across the black, silent afternoon. Clett's thoughts turned again to the case against Ronnie Rust.

* * *

At the Pickaquoy swimming pool, a patch of late sunshine streamed in from the large glass wall, reflecting bright patches from the water's surface on to the high roof of the pool. Ronnie Rust slowly inhaled and bent his knees and sprung from the side of the pool. He lifted, airborne for a moment, and he felt himself enter the blue water. The initial cold was soon replaced with a comfortable sensation that enveloped him. He quickly fell into the rhythm of his strokes. One length crawl, one length breaststroke, to be repeated, again and again. He enjoyed the feeling of the movement of the water around him, supporting his weight and encompassing his body in this enclosed void. Even the sounds, the shouts of children and the magnified conversations, amplified by the reflective surfaces of the surrounding glass walls, were but a muffled nothing to Ronnie Rust as he counted off the strokes in isolation, each practiced and experienced; each repeated by choice, and each in its way, inevitable. After about twenty lengths, each stroke became an attempt at a perfect movement, special kind of tiny habit, becoming a small life, each stroke becoming a new start, a new beginning, both new and repeated, each one lived as a complete rounded thing, independent from the stroke before, separate from the stroke to come.

Ronnie Rust used this time as a means to separate himself from his day-to-day problems and concerns, repeatedly propelling himself from one side of the pool to the other. Unknowingly, he counted the strokes and the lengths, but despite these numbers, in this timeless space he was to swim an infinite number of lengths, savouring each stroke, each stroke a tiny eternity.

He dried himself off and, on the way out to the car park, he nodded to two boys running past with their kit bags, sliding on a frozen puddle. They were about ten years old, their shirts blowing in the wind. They had red faces; their trainers unlaced.

"Hello James, and if it isn't wee Jessie, Janie Shearer's wee girl. How are the two of you?"

"Fine Mister Rust. We're going for a swim."

"Aye well, the water is not warm."

"That's ok Mister Rust. The cold doesn't bother us."

The children giggled and pushed each other across the car park. Rust smiled.

"Jessie, tell your Mum I'll see her tomorrow."

Jessie and James stopped and watched the lights on Rust's silver BMW flash in welcome. The number plate said RUS 5.

Rust switched on the heated seat and looked at his phone. He had a missed call from his lawyer. He called back.

"George, how are tricks?"

"Ronnie, I think we can rubbish some of the evidence at the trial tomorrow."

"Good news. I expected nothing less from George Barr, Writer to the Signet."

There was a short pause before Barr continued. "We may have the witness sorted. Also, If I can get Clett into the stand, I can question his motives. As for the victim, I think she'll be too traumatised to give evidence."

"I hope nothing underhand has happened to that poor girl. Geraldine was my right-hand man, you know."

There was silence at the other end of the phone before George Barr spoke again. "My main concern is the DNA evidence. The blood on the sweatshirt they took from you is damning."

"Look. I pay you good money. Do your job. If you have a problem, just go into court and see what comes up. It was you told me that most acquittals are because someone makes a mistake. I pay you because you are lucky, George Barr, Writer to the Signet."

"I'm not sure on this one, Ronnie. You should prepare yourself."

CHAPTER FIVE

$$Cu-\overset{\displaystyle \overset{OH}{\diagup}}{\underset{\displaystyle \diagdown}{C}}=O$$

OH

verdigris

T-Block, RAF Whale Head
Friday 13th November 1942

"Observe as I demonstrate the function of the earth wand."

Henry Long rolled his eyes.

"I am aware that you know all this, Private Long, but we must jump through these hoops at the instruction of our superiors, so let's get this over with and we can return to more important matters. Let's start, shall we?"

Sergeant Cameron placed his hand on the steel cabinet, now silent in the middle of the room.

"The Type T.3026 transmitter was built by Metropolitan-Vickers…"

The transmitter was housed in a large grey steel enclosure, the height of a man. Normally, it would hum with life, the noise of the oil diffusion vacuum pump and the fans and the plumbing for the water-cooled valve bubbling away. But now, the transmitter lay dormant, its doors splayed open, exposing its organs. With no power applied, the silent transmitter contained high voltage components that could accumulate charge from the static electricity in the air. Indeed, the huge capacitors held enough electrical charge to kill a man.

Henry ground his teeth at the sound of Cameron's Canadian accent. He thought of his humiliation in front of Charlotte in the NAAFI. She would see him for a fool. The shame overwhelmed him. Cameron's voice drifted into his consciousness, floating among his thoughts.

"As you know, this is the earth wand, otherwise known as a grounding rod."

Cameron held the copper device by its Bakelite sheath. The

earth wand was shaped like a shepherd's crook, a yard long with some oxide staining, attached by a length of covered wire to a grounded earth point, bolted securely at the base of the transmitter cabinet.

"We must check these bolts are secure each week. If they are not secured, the earth wand becomes ineffective. It will not protect us against the high residual charge; lethal static voltages that can reach many thousands of volts. We offer the wand to each of these hotspots every time we carry out maintenance, touching each of these points to discharge them. Thus, we can continue working in safety. The earth wand is your friend. You will be in no danger if you use the earth wand."

Cameron indicated the hot spots in the transmitter, touching each of them with the wand.

At the last point, the wand came into contact with a hotspot, there was a crack and a flash of blue light as the energy was discharged.

Sergeant Cameron smiled at the uncommunicative, sulky young man in front of him. He had a soft spot for him. Who hadn't been moody as a young man? At his age, he had new responsibilities, when he had to face the world as a man, especially now, in this uncertain war. He smiled; Henry sneered back.

The two men spent an hour replacing the heaters in the power tetrode. These valves were unique in that it was possible to replace the inner components of the valve without removing the entire tube. The heaters warmed the cathode, causing it to emit streams of ions, plasma that accelerated towards the anode, from where the electromagnetic energy was fed to the aerials, out into the ether. Henry put his hand on the cabinet, feeling the warm steel under his fingertips. Inside, within the thermionic valve, this stream of ions, this plasma, was to him something that indicated the possibility of the infinite. He had become convinced that this was the same energy that he observed in the aurora borealis, above him in the night sky. Here in T-Block, these little glass bottles contained in their dancing blue glow the natural force of the universe.

They restored the transmitter to service, starting the power-up sequence. Cameron and Henry 'conditioned' the new filament, slowly raising the voltage on the heater, increasing the vacuum inside the valve, while priming the water-cooling pump, recording readings as they went. Forty-five minutes later, the valve was working at full power, a full potential of thirty-five thousand volts. At this voltage, the valve shone its blue light from the imprisoned plasma, illuminating the whole room. Henry smiled to himself, bathed in its aura, this single little merry dancer, tamed, contained in its glass envelope. Now, the transmitter humming and sucking and gurgling and pulsing, alive; existing only to create the wall of radio waves that protected the country.

Burgh Road Police Station, Kirkwall
Wednesday 15th December 2010

Sent today at 11:20:21
From: Irene Seath
Subject: ORK/2010/12/14/Lopness SPSA SOCO
Preliminary observations
To: Roland Clett (Insp); Margaret McPhee (CI)
Cc: Norman Clouston (Sgt); Sanja Dilpit (SOCO)

Good Morning Inspector. Please see below our initial observations concerning the body found on Sanday at coordinates 59.277920, -2.420327.
The remains have been dispatched to Aberdeen for post-mortem and results will be circulated when complete. Our findings are that the deceased is male, approximately 90 years old. No obvious wound, punctures or injuries apart from burns on both hands which must have happened as a young man. The deceased showed signs of advanced osteoarthritis, particularly in his hands.
Cause of death not confirmed, but a metal one litre thermos flask was found nearby that had contained ether (Diethyl Ether [Ethoxyethane] Laboratory Grade with Stabiliser). It has been suggested that this constituted part of an 'exit kit' for the self-application of ether. If this is the case, no plastic bag or other means of application have yet been found. As you observed, there was a strong odour of ether from the body.
A small dish containing a grey powder-like substance and some bread appear to have been placed on the body post mortem; it is unlikely that the dish would have stayed in place as the subject expired. The powder has been identified as a primitive salt compound. This powder may yield more information. Following spectrum

analysis, we should be able to identify isotopes that may allow us to discover its source. The bread is white sliced bread, texturally similar to standard supermarket white bread. We estimate that it was probably bought on or around 12th December. It has been sent for grain and mould analysis.

The deceased was dressed in a funeral shroud. No other items of clothing were found in the vicinity. Beneath the shroud, the subject was wearing a tunic made of goat skin, the hairs on the inside. This had irritated the skin of the deceased to the extent that tit was red and swollen, the skin broken in many places. We believe that he was wearing this hair shirt to cause permanent discomfort.

Another update tomorrow at 11.00 as per SPSA SLA (2008), but please get in touch if any queries arise.
Regards
Irene Seath (SOCO) 07222 176687
Sanja Dilpit. (SOCO) 07222 176688

* * *

Clett entered the foyer of the Burgh Road Police Station. Nancie Keldie was the duty desk officer, dealing with a busy waiting room. She leaned forward.

"Excuse me Inspector, someone to see you."

He looked up from his phone, around the waiting room. Keldie pointed to a frail figure in the corner who looked up as Clett approached.

"Excuse me, how can I help you?"

The young woman's eyes flickered around the room, darted back in the direction of Clett and then down again.

"Eh, I...I don't know if you remember me, I'm Geraldine Work."

"Geraldine, of course. I was expecting to see you at court tomorrow. How are you?"

Clett spoke softly, hiding his shock at the sight of the young woman. He had not recognised her; she looked twenty years older, her skin was grey, her eyes sunk in her skull. Her hair was thin and lank, her clothes dirty. She had a twitch and blinked continuously. Not six months ago this fragile woman had been successfully running the Fraction nightclub for Ronnie Rust when she was viciously assaulted by him. Clett knew she had been hospitalised, but now she was unrecognisable. He could tell very well how she was.

"Oh, I'm ok Inspector."

"Come on inside, Geraldine. Can I get you a cup of tea?"

"No thanks Inspector. I have my Red Bull."

Her hands shook as she took a small sip from the can, holding it with both hands. She continued twitching and couldn't make eye contact. He nodded to Nancy Keldie.

"We'll use interview room two."

Nancie Keldie looked on as Clett took Geraldine by the elbow.

"Sorry, Geraldine this is the only quiet room we have just now."

She stood, holding on to the side of the table, staying near the door. Clett touched her arm and she let herself be guided to the seat where she perched, slouching forward.

"Geraldine, what's happened?"

"It kind of...just...I, em..."

Her voice trailed away as she bit her nails – already down to the quick.

"Is it the court case tomorrow? Are you upset about that?"

"Yes, No....It's just that..."

She blinked her eyes tight.

"Why don't you tell me the whole story. When did you get out of hospital?"

"Eh...I don't know, in May sometime, maybe."

"Where have you been staying?"

"Back at the flat...until...until this."

Geraldine rocked slowly back and forth.

Clett placed his hand on her shoulder. "Take your time. Is it about the court case tomorrow?"

Geraldine shook her head.

"Is it your son, is it about wee Raymond?"

Geraldine's shoulders jerked, and she nodded.

"Where is he?"

"He...I...we just...they took..."

Her words lost, she blinked away tears.

"Ok. Someone has taken him?"

Geraldine nodded.

"Ok. Who has taken Raymond, Geraldine?"

"The so…cial s…" she sobbed.

"The social services?"

"Yes."

"Why have the social services taken your little boy?"

Geraldine paused and answered clearly: "Because I am a bad mother."

She sniffed.

"Geraldine, you have had a lot to deal with recently."

"No. No. No, I must deserve this. I am a bad person."

"Geraldine. Are you seeing any professional help; a counsellor perhaps?"

"Not really, no, I don't need one."

Clett paused to let her breathe.

"Ok. Let's take one thing at a time. When was Raymond removed?"

"Last night."

"Who was there?"

"Eh, a few people. a policewoman, a social worker, I think. They had a piece of paper. They said a sheriff signed it."

"And where is Raymond now?"

"They wouldn't tell me. A safe place, they said."

"Ok, it looks like he has been placed under a Child Protection Order and transferred to a Place of Safety. Did they use these words?"

"Yes, maybe."

"Ok. Did they say why?"

"I don't know. There were all these people, it was…confusing."

"Did they give you a copy of the warrant?"

"I think so. I don't know. They gave me this."

Geraldine took some crumpled torn sheets of paper from her pocket. Clett scanned the social worker's preliminary report.

Unheated flat – Raymond wearing wholly inappropriate clothing – Child's skin freezing to the touch – No toys. Home largely unfurnished – Raymond and his Mother share a single mattress with no bedding. No pyjamas – Raymond seriously underweight. Child searched

*in the pockets of the social workers for food – flat
extremely unhygienic – dirt and damp on walls –
Kitchen full of unwashed dishes – Dirty clothes
strewn around flat – bath stained and dirty – Old
crisp packets, sugary drinks cans and energy
drinks littering the flat – no evidence of
drug/alcohol abuse.*

And the concluding narrative:

*A Child Protection Order is necessary
to meet Raymond's needs. His physical safety, his
health, and his emotional and mental stimulation
needs are not being met. Ms Geraldine Work
(mother) is unable to prioritise her son's needs
above her own. Raymond Work is to be removed
to a Place of Safety.*

Clett had seen this kind of neglect in the past. A loving parent overwhelmed by debt, domestic violence, or worry, resulting in the need of the social services to protect the child. Geraldine was not an uncaring parent; he clearly recognised the symptoms of post-traumatic stress following the assault on her by Rust.

"Ok Geraldine, I think the next step will be a series of children's hearings and other meetings. Raymond has been removed from your care to protect him. You need help yourself. Until you can get better, you will not be able to look after him. It is important that you engage with social work. They will work out a program to try to get you and Raymond back together."

"You mean I can get him back, Inspector Clett?"

"Possibly, but only if you work with the social workers. You must never miss a contact visit; you must turn up for every meeting they organise, and you must cooperate fully. If they say you should talk to other professionals, you must do so. The first thing you must do is clean up the flat. Social Work will help you there."

"If I do this, I get my wee Raymond back?"

"If you can do what the Social Work say is necessary, there is every likelihood you will get him back."

"So, when can he come home?"

"I can't say. It depends on how long it takes to get you back on your feet. It could be a long time, a year or more."

"A year…"

Geraldine started crying again, not making a sound.

"But you should be able to see him during contact visits. The more you cooperate, the better the chances of seeing him more regularly."

"But a year. I don't know if I can keep it together for that long."

"Geraldine, when is your next meeting?"

"They said something about a second hearing tomorrow."

Clett paused.

"You do know that your assault case is tomorrow, the case against Ronnie Rust."

Geraldine made eye contact with Clett for the first time.

"What am I going to do? You said I had to attend the meetings, or they would keep Raymond away from me."

She put her head in her hands, rocking back and forward.

"Geraldine, you have to attend the court hearing. I will get in touch with Social Work and the Children's Panel Reporter and explain the situation."

"I don't know, Inspector. Maybe I should ask Mister Rust for help?"

Clett took a sharp intake of breath. He was dumbstruck.

"What? No! You can't. After what he did to you. Geraldine. Look at me. Tomorrow he is to be tried for a vicious, unprovoked attack on you. The case will be seriously jeopardised if they hear that you had approached him. That is the very worst thing you can do."

Geraldine shrugged her shoulders, sipping from her tin of Red Bull. She twitched.

"I just thought he could help. You know, put in a word for me. He knows people."

"Geraldine, don't go near that man. I'll talk to Social Work and I'll get back to you. What's your mobile number?"

"It's, eh...I lost it."

"Your home phone number?"

"My landline was cut off."

There was a knock, and Nancie Keldie put her head around the door.

"Inspector – more information from Constable Skea about the Sanday situation."

"Ok constable, I'll be out in a minute."

Clett moved closer to Geraldine, ignoring her body odour.

"Wait here while I make a call. I'll tell them about your court appearance tomorrow and we'll get some help for you. Just don't, whatever you do, get in touch with Ronnie Rust."

She nodded vigorously, raised her drink to her mouth and twitched.

"Promise me?"

* * *

After Geraldine's departure, Clett unfolded a photocopied letter and started reading.

> *To David Hume*
> *1 St David's Street*
> *Edinburgh*
> *May 14th 1756*
> *My Dear friend.*
> *I have to inform you that I have found your fine Treatise on Human Nature to be a spur to my own little philosophies. In particular, I have been thinking about dreams, and their place in the workings of Shame in the moral mind. You write of Shame as a passion, and I would like to present the contrasting view that Shame is a sentiment. The evidence for this is manifest in the higher animals and primates. When a dog transgresses in the home, one can distinguish a look of shame in the knowledge of the transgression. This look is a sunken lowered head, and the tail between its legs. Many years ago, on my grand tour, I visited Gibraltar and observed the apes on the rock. It was apparent that they had rules that they kept as a group. These rules were their laws, and when an individual acted outside these rules, say stealing food from a more superior ape, that individual displayed a look of shame, and either tried to hide its act, or run*

away, but always returned to the group, knowing that punishment awaited.

We have a natural balance of sentiment to which we invisibly pursue to the goal of a healthy mind that is the result of our satisfactory engagement with our society. Shame is the internal mechanism that regulates this balance.

I now turn to dreams. Dreams can prepare us for danger. We need an optimum level of danger in our lives. If we do not have that level of danger, our subconscious invents danger in our dream lives.

The same goes for other factors in life. If there is a deficit of love, passion, misery, hatred, affection, or despair, our own subconscious balances this out in our dream world and equilibrium is maintained.

And, so to the privacy of shame. Each of us is ashamed of something we have done, or something we have said. Whether or not we said or whether we did the correct thing, we know that there was something about that transaction that resulted from an unbalance of our moral engagement with our society. We would not speak about this thing in an open space. Our shame is private and will always be so.

When our shame becomes public, we become Criminal. Before that time, before we become Criminal, we are ashamed. Shame is the hidden bond between Civility and Criminality. Shame is the reminder that we are all susceptible to those actions that may be deemed Criminal.

I should like to discuss further my notions of a vocabulary of Shame, the compass of which is the measure of our Publick Moralitie. I shall think on such and

write to you again.
Yr. Humble Servant,
Arch. Clett of Canmore.

* * *

At the door of the Foveran, Clett and Christine kicked the snow from their feet and a young man showed them to a seat. As they scanned the menu, Clett saw three people sitting at the other side of the restaurant. He recognised Ronnie Rust immediately.

"Christine, I'm sorry, we can't stay here."

"Whyever not?"

"Don't look around, but Ronnie Rust is sitting over there."

"Can't we even go out for a meal?"

"I'm sorry, Christine. I'll make it up to you."

As Clett helped Christine on with her coat, Ronnie Rust waved, grinning at them.

"Hello, Inspector, and the lovely Mrs Inspector Clett."

Clett glared at Rust as he and Christine turned towards the door, apologising to the waiter. As they were leaving, they saw the face of Janie Shearer laughing, sitting across from Ronnie Rust. Clett didn't recognise the third person, dressed in an expensive suit; tanned. Obviously not from Orkney.

Out in the car park, Clett and Christine squeezed past a limousine, the driver wearing dark glasses. Beside him, a smart woman in a black business suit played with her phone.

"What on earth was Janie Shearer doing sharing a meal with Ronnie Rust? Are they in a relationship?"

"Can't see it, but they seemed to be enjoying each other's company. And what about that person sitting with them? Did you see his shoes?"

"Aye; and he didn't get that tan at Waulkmill Bay! Maybe they're just using each other. Rust making connections with the press that will be helpful if he is successful in becoming a councillor, and Janie keeping track of this dangerous man for a story, perhaps."

"Jealous?"

"Of course not."

"Because we all know your past with Janie Shearer."

"How many times do I have to tell you? I have no past with

Janie Shearer."

"So you say."

"Let's just go to The Kirkwall Hotel. They've got partains[3]."

* * *

Geraldine Work went into the telephone box next to the tourist office at the waterfront, put some ten pence pieces into the phone and dialled. She waited as the dial tone repeated itself twice. He always let it ring twice. There was a click as the phone was lifted.

"Hello, Mister Rust?"

"This is he."

"This is Geraldine, Geraldine Work."

Rust paused, smiling.

"Hello Geraldine. It's so good to hear from you. How are you?"

"Oh, I'm fine Mister Rust."

"Come on now Geraldine, call me Ronnie. We've known each other long enough."

"Ok, em, ok Ronnie."

"That's better, what can I do for you?"

"Well, I'm not sure. Things haven't gone that well for me recently."

"I'm very sorry to hear that, Geraldine."

"Yes, and the worst of it is that they have taken my wee Raymond into care."

"That's terrible, Geraldine. Who remove a child from a loving parent?"

"Well, I haven't exactly been the perfect mother recently."

"Who is a perfect parent, Geraldine? Who can put their hands up and say that? Come on now, Geraldine, tell me everything."

"Well Mister Rust, it's about tomorrow. They say that I have to go to a hearing tomorrow about what happens to Raymond."

"The Social Services?"

"Uh, huh."

"Tomorrow; yes, I see."

"Yes. And I am supposed to be at court for this…"

---

[3] partains – crabs.

Geraldine paused, "…this other thing."

"Yes. I understand, Geraldine. This must all be very difficult for you."

"I don't know what to do, Mister Rust. Ronnie. Inspector Clett says that I should go to court and he will sort out the Social Services. But if I do that, they might not let me have Raymond back because I didn't turn up. Oh God. I just don't know what to do."

Rust smiled.

"Geraldine; relax. You know what I always say; one problem at a time, one day at a time. You have to ask yourself what's important to you? Your future with your son or your appearance in court tomorrow? It won't be the end of the world if you don't turn up at court. The Sheriff will merely adjourn for your attendance. You'll probably be sitting around all day doing nothing anyway."

"Do you think so?"

"Yes, I do think so, Geraldine, but you must follow what your heart tells you."

"But the children's hearing might still keep Raymond away from me."

"Well let's just leave that for tomorrow, why don't we. I'll see if I can't make a call or two."

"Oh, Mister Rust, could you, you have been so helpful. I am so glad I phoned."

"That's no problem at all, Geraldine."

Rust put his mobile phone on the coffee table; a voice came from the kitchen:

"Cup of tea, Ronald?"

"Yes please, Auntie Brenda."

Rust returned to *The Science of the Inner You* by Gerauld Surrmann. Once more, he quickly found that sentence:

Are you afraid of sex?

Reading these words, his palms became sweaty. He wiped them on his trousers and tried to focus on the author's narrative; but all he could focus on were those words that went round and round in his head. How did Gerauld Surrmann have this insight? How did he know? Rust was fearful of what else this man would say. What other secrets did Surrmann know about Ronnie Rust?

Auntie Brenda placed a cup of steaming tea on a mat on the coffee table.

"There you go, Ronald."

Rust shifted uncomfortably on the sofa, hiding the book under a cushion.

"Thank you, Auntie Brenda."

"What's that you are reading?"

"It's nothing really."

"My, Ronald, you are such a clever boy. You're always reading. All these books; and you are so successful, too. You know, I'm so proud of you."

She bent over and kissed him on the forehead.

Rust wriggled uncomfortably on the sofa.

"Yes, Auntie Brenda."

CHAPTER SIX

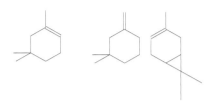

turpentine

Lopness, Sanday
Saturday 14th November 1942

There was a sharp chill in the air, but the momentary winter sun bathed the whole archipelago; anyone who stepped outside in those few minutes that morning was instantly warmed. Charlotte walked west on the path toward the Isbister farm, past the doocot and the sound of cooing. Smoke belched in lumps from a small bonfire in the yard. A large woman wearing a headscarf and wellington boots was throwing things on the fire. Charlotte observed her coming and going from a stone-built outhouse, carrying paintings towards the fire. A pile was already burning, and she was about to throw more on to the little inferno.

"I say, why are you burning your paintings?"

The woman glanced at Charlotte and threw another picture on the flames.

"Because it's good for the soul, dear."

Without looking at them, she tossed two more on to the fire.

"Yes, good for the soul."

Charlotte came closer. They seemed to be fine pieces of work, all of a similar size, about fourteen inches by eight. Some had painted arrows added to indicate a point of balance almost tipping the image on its side. One was a landscape with strong aerial perspective, making more distant objects appear to have a blue hue. One had what might have been musical notation, or script, or was it lines of Morse code? The flames consumed the image before Charlotte could decide.

"Madam, please do not burn these lovely things. Even I can see that these are fine works."

"Can you now?"

The woman paused. She held a larger piece, about to place it on the fire. It appeared to be a burnt umber representation of a standing stone, the painted texture of granite and coloured lichen, even more striking in the strong morning sun.

"May I look at it?"

The woman held up the painting.

"What, this thing?"

"Yes, I would, rather; if you don't mind."

Charlotte took the image and held it away from the glare of the sun, into the shadow of the outhouse. She examined the painted surface, holding the picture close to see the detail. On examination, it showed the natural texture of the rock, articulated in oils. Charlotte touched the surface, surprised that it was so smooth, and not the sharp gritty feeling of stone.

"Gosh, this is lovely. Gesso, yes?"

"Yes, gesso, dear."

"Must have taken ages."

Charlotte looked at the initials at the bottom.

"M.I. You are M.I.?"

"Mergret Isbister, of Lopness."

"How do you do? My name is Charlotte Hall, of Shere; you know, in Surrey."

"Is it? Well, Charlotte Hall of Shere-in-Surrey, I am very pleased to meet you."

The two women shook hands warmly.

"Mrs Isbister, I still don't understand, why are you burning your paintings?"

"I am having a clear out. Call me Mergret."

"But how do you select which ones to burn?"

"At random, dear, at random."

Charlotte gasped.

"But Mrs…Mergret, how can you do that? These are beautiful."

Mergret returned to the studio. Charlotte stood at the door as the older woman selected another painting.

"Is that ether I can smell?"

"Turpentine, methinks."

"Oh, yes; of course."

Mergret squeezed past Charlotte.

"Are you burning them because of the war?"

"Why do you say that?"

"I don't know, maybe you think art has no place during wartime; all this horribleness; bombs, rationing, people being sent to all sorts of places, far from home."

"You mean places like Orkney? No, dear, quite the contrary. At times like this, art nourishes our humanity."

"But why do you burn them? It is so upsetting to see you destroy these lovely things."

"It's complicated. Do you paint?"

"No. My father does; watercolours, mostly."

"Well, Charlotte, isn't it?"

"Yes, from Shere."

"From Shere, yes."

"Charlotte, from Shere. I'll let you in on a little secret. Artists struggle to control their work. You have control over it only while you are making it. Once a piece is complete, once others see it, they change the narrative; it takes away my ownership of the piece."

"You mean, you are maintaining control over your work, perhaps before it is seen by the public?"

"In a way, yes. The monstrous public."

"Isn't that rather harsh?"

"Not really. I love people to have my work, but I must keep a degree of control over what I do."

Charlotte smiled and looked at her watch.

"Must dash. Back to work, you know."

"Good girl. Keep up the good toil; do come again."

"Thank you, Mergret. I'd love to."

Mergret paused, examining the still life in her hands, and placed it back with the others on the floor of her studio.

"Probably enough for today."

Watergate Sheriff Court, Kirkwall
Thursday 16th December 2010

Ronnie Rust stood in the sleet deposits at the front of the Sheriff Court at Watergate, peering out to the Spire of St Magnus cathedral supporting the steel grey canopy. The wind blew the streetlights rattling against the dim sky, illuminating intersecting cones of swirling snow, punctuating the dreich air. He was joined by George Barr, Writer to the Signet, who lit a cigarette.

"Morning George."

Rust rubbed his hands together.

"And who's the presiding judge today?"

"The Honorary Sheriff, Charlie Sinclair."

"Ah, my old chum. That's good news for me, wouldn't you say, George Barr, Writer to the Signet?"

Barr puffed on the cigarette and blew the smoke out into the snow.

"It is highly unusual to have an Honorary Sheriff presiding over a case like this; highly unusual."

Rust smiled and winked at Barr. "Funny how these things turn out, wouldn't you say?"

Rust stood straight, immune to the wind and weather. Barr kicked the snow from his shoes, extinguishing his cigarette before opening the double doors for his client to enter.

"Do you know the word scurrilous, George? It is from the Latin scurrilis. It means derisive — my word for the day."

"Yes, Ronnie."

Barr flicked the cigarette end to the ground and stubbed it out with his toe.

Inside the courtroom, Sigurd Rostung approached Clett, his gown billowing in the draught from the open door.

"Look Roland dear chap, I'm sorry, but this might not turn out as we had hoped; the court may deem our witness evidence inadmissible."

"Aye Sigurd, but the blood type evidence should be Ok."

"As far as I know, but you should be aware, it won't be as straightforward as we had anticipated."

"Where's Geraldine? I gave her a phone; she's not answering."

On entering the warm courtroom, Ronnie Rust smiled, warmly shaking hands with the half-dozen or so people in the public gallery. Some clapped, and he raised a hand in recognition. Clett watched from the gallery, seething at the man's gall. Rust sat down with his lawyer as the other court officials took their places. They stood as The Honorary Sheriff Charlie Sinclair entered. After some preliminaries, the clerk read the charge.

"Ronald Gerald Rust, you are charged that on the 27th April, 2010, at approximately four-ten in the afternoon, at the Fraction nightclub, Kirkwall, you did assault Geraldine Anne Work, care of Kirkwall Police Station, to her severe injury, permanent disfigurement and to the danger of her life. How do you plead?"

Rust smiled gently and shook his head from side to side. "Not Guilty, your lordship, absolutely not guilty."

There was a buzz of approval from the public gallery. The Honorary Sheriff Charlie Sinclair caught the Rust's eye and glanced down at his gavel. He coughed loudly for silence; nodded sagely and took a note. Sigurd Rostung, Procurator Fiscal stood at his table, gripping the lapels of his gown.

"The Crown would like to call the first witness for the prosecution to the stand, Mr Bruce Drever."

A man in his twenties wearing a new suit stepped into the stand and took the oath.

"Mr Drever, can you explain the court what you saw on the afternoon of the twenty-seventh of April at the service entrance of the Fraction Nightclub in Kirkwall?"

"Yes. As I passed the lane leading to the entrance, a silver BMW accelerated out into the street towards me."

"Thank you. Did you observe the driver of the car?"

"Yes."

"Can you point him out please?"

"He is the man in the dock."

Bruce Drever pointed towards Ronnie Rust. Rust shook his head.

"Mr Drever, how do you know that it was this man who drove the car?"

"I will never forget the look on his face; he was covered in blood. He aimed straight for me."

"Thank you, Mr Drever."

The Honorary Sheriff looked to George Barr.

"Mister Barr, do you wish to cross examine?"

"Not at this point, my Lord."

"Very well. Mister Drever, you may stand down, but you may be called again to give further evidence."

Sigurd Rostung waited for the young man to leave the courtroom.

"My Lord, I should now like to present the state's evidence in the form of the forensic report on this sweatshirt, reference SPSA/144B/10 dated the 13th June 2010. I wish to call to the stand, Scene of Crimes Officer Sanja Dilpet."

Sanja briskly took her place and affirmed. Rostung approached the stand.

"Can you please tell the court your role as regards this case."

"I am a Scene of Crimes Officer working for SPSA, the Scottish Police Support Services. I examined the forensic evidence supplied to me by Northern Constabulary in respect of this case."

"What was this evidence?"

"It was a bloodstained sweatshirt."

The clerk held up a sweatshirt in a shrink-wrapped bag. The logo FCUK a watermark in the brown staining of the old blood that saturated it.

"I would like to present the court with the state's prosecution evidence reference SPSA/144A/10. It belonged to the defendant, Mister Ronald Rust. Ms Dilpit, can you describe to the court your findings concerning this sweatshirt?"

"I examined the blood deposits on the item of clothing. They were found to be blood type O."

"I would like to advise the court that this blood type is that of Geraldine Work."

George Barr stood:

"Objection, my Lord."

"Upheld. Have you more than this, Mr Rostung?"

"Indeed I do, my Lord."

"Carry on."

"Miss Dilpit, did you carry out any further analysis on the blood on the sweatshirt?"

"Yes. As documented in the forensic report, we carried out a DNA analysis, concluding that the blood found on the sweatshirt matched samples taken from Miss Geraldine Work."

"So, for the benefit of the court, what can you say about these blood samples?"

"We can state with a very high degree of probability that these blood deposits were from Geraldine Work."

"Thank you, Ms Dilpit. No more questions."

The Honorary Sheriff Charlie Sinclair nodded to Sanja.

"Does the defence counsel wish to cross examine?"

"If it so please, my Lord."

George Barr blew his nose and placed his handkerchief in his pocket.

"Miss Dilpit, you stated that the blood was type O."

"That is correct."

"What would you say if I said that the blood type of the defendant, Mister Ronald Rust, is also type O?"

"The brief given to SPSA was to identify the blood type on the sweatshirt. SPSA do not engage in investigative activities."

"Quite."

Barr took a few steps around the courtroom in silence. He went to the table, picking up the forensic report, thumbing through it. The Sheriff cleared his throat.

"Mr Barr, have you any more questions?"

Barr scanned the report again.

"Not at this time, my Lord, but I may wish to re-examine the witness."

"Good, I think we shall break for lunch."

* * *

"Ur ye no havin' lunch, Inspector?"

"Hello, Sanja. No. I'll get something when I get home."

"Trial not going your way?"

"Can't say. You've done your bit. See how things pan out."

Clett kicked away some slush from the steps.

"Whit ur they wee bits o' paper you keep lookin' at?"

"These? They're photocopies of letters from an eighteenth-century Orkney man of ideas, Archibald Clett. He corresponded with major figures of the day – Benjamin Franklin, David Hume, Voltaire."

"Wow! Is he well known?"

"Not really. He wrote only one book, 'Upon the Sentiment of Morality',"

"Archibald Clett?. Would he be a relation, then?"

"Not that I know of."

"Ye seem tae spend a lot o' time reading them."

"I'm transcribing them. Maybe I'll try to get them published."

"Dae ye no find them a distraction from the work?"

"Quite the opposite. I find they settle my mind."

"Ah ken whit ye mean. Ah dae sudokus ma'sel."

"Sometimes Archibald's letters surprise me with their relevance."

"How's that?"

"Take this letter. It's about his involvement in a project to chart the coastline of Orkney for the mapmaker Mackenzie, who created some of the first charts for the British Admiralty. They started with a length of chain on a frozen loch. This gave them a precise meridian from which they triangulated to form a dataset that allowed them to create a chart. In this case, we need a similar meridian from which to benchmark our own evidence."

"The plastic bag fur the ether?"

"Or the identity of the old man."

Sanja looked at the cross written script on the page.

"A' that fae they wee squiggles?"

* * *

As the court filled, George Barr peered at his laptop, comparing the contents of the screen with the paper forensic report. He scratched his ear and fiddled with the computer. Then he smiled, leaned back in his chair and stretched. The Honorary Sheriff Charlie Sinclair entered, bowed, and took his seat. The court settled as he addressed Sigurd Rostung.

"Does the prosecution wish to call any more witnesses?"

Sigurd looked across the gallery at Clett, who was examining at his phone. He shook his head at Rostung.

"My Lord, for the defence, we had intended to call Miss Geraldine Work, but it would appear that Miss Work is currently too distressed, and does not want to testify at this time, but we may wish to call her later for re-examination, if it please the court."

"This is very unusual, Mr Rostung; perhaps an adjournment?"

"I am grateful for the court's latitude, my Lord. However, in order to avoid wasting the court's time further, may I suggest that in lieu of the absence of this witness, I would like to submit her statement as evidence and examine Miss Work later. We are confident that she will attend tomorrow."

The Honorary Sheriff Charlie Sinclair avoided Rust's look, avoiding his smile.

"I repeat, Mr Rostung, this is extremely unusual. I am minded to accept from the defence counsel a request for a motion of mistrial in this case, since the prosecution appears not to be in a position to marshal its resources. Perhaps the defence counsel has an opinion. Mr Barr?"

"If I may confer with my client, my Lord?"

"As you wish, Mr Barr."

Barr leaned over to Ronnie Rust, who whispered to Barr; he leaned back, smiling.

"My Lord, my client wishes it to be known that in the full and open interest of justice being done, we have no objection to Miss Work being recalled as a prosecution witness when she is fit and able."

"That is uncommonly generous of your client, Mr Barr."

"Indeed, my Lord. It is the nature of the man, and of our confidence in his innocence in this matter."

There was a murmur from the public gallery; Sigurd Rostung shrugged his shoulders at Clett. The Honorary Sheriff tapped his gavel on the block.

"So, to the defence evidence, if you please, Mr Barr."

"As you wish, my Lord."

George Barr took the floor.

"I would like to recall Mr Bruce Drever to the stand."

The young man was led across the courtroom. Outside, seagulls called to each other across the cold sky.

"Mr Drever, you stated that you saw a BMW leave the site of the Fraction nightclub at around four-ten in the afternoon on Tuesday, the twenty-seventh of April, this year."

"That's right. It accelerated towards me. I had to get out of the way."

"And what was the registration marking on the BMW?"

"I didn't get a chance to see it. The car was moving very..."

"So, you can't specifically identify the BMW as that of Ronnie Rust? I would remind the jury that this vehicle has the very distinctive registration RUS5. We saw the photographs presented by the prosecution. Mr Drever, I ask you again, did you see the registration?"

"No to be honest, I couldn't put my hand on my heart and say that was the registration, but he was driving it."

"I see. Who was driving the car Mr Drever?"

"That man in the dock, Ronnie Rust."

"Had you met Mister Rust before the events we are talking

about?"

"No."

"Do you know my client Ronald Gerald Rust?"

"No. I know who he is, but I don't know him personally."

"I see, but you think that you are able to identify him as the driver of the BMW?"

"Yes."

"How is that Mr Drever?"

"Because he drove straight at me. His sweatshirt was covered in blood. I saw him."

"You *think* you saw my client Mister Rust?"

"I did see him. I saw him in broad daylight."

"Mr Drever, do you remember the weather on the twenty-seventh of April?"

"No."

"If I told you that it was very sunny, would you be surprised at that?"

"No. I suppose not."

"More specifically, the sun was coming from the south, and that it had been raining earlier in the day."

"If you say so."

"I have here a map showing the entrance to the Fraction nightclub. Can you please point to where you were standing?"

"Here, at Burnmouth Road."

"Looking east towards the exit from the car park?"

"Yes, I suppose so."

"And this was at ten past four."

"Yes."

"My team had some photographs taken in this area with a similar car. I have them here. Item A in the defence bundle, my Lord."

George Barr passed the photos to the Clerk and to Sigurd Rostung.

"You will discern from these photographs that there is a very significant amount of glare from the windscreen of the car, and from the sun reflecting off the wet road surface.

There was a mumble of comment as the clerk passed the photographs to the Sheriff.

"This exercise was repeated around fifteen times at times plus and minus half an hour either side of the time in question and in similar weather conditions. I submit the Meteorological Office records for both the 27th April, and the days of our reconstruction: Item B, my Lord. They evidence the weather conditions on the day."

Barr put his hands in his pockets and faced the witness box.

"The defence counsel assert that these photographs demonstrate glare from the windscreen that would mean that that the driver could not be seen from the where you were standing. Do you have any comment Mr Drever?"

"I saw him. His sweatshirt was covered in blood. He pointed the car at me."

"I am sorry Mr Drever, but your testimony is not consistent with the photographs we have presented. I would suggest to the court that this witness testimony is not reliable."

"But I saw him."

"That will be all from the defence."

The Honorary Sheriff Charlie Sinclair tapped his gavel.

"Mr Rostung, do you wish a rebuttal?"

"Obliged, my Lord. Mr Drever, for the Jury, I would like you to repeat your testimony. Did you see Ronald Rust driving the silver BMW away from the car park at the rear of the Fraction nightclub?"

"Yes I did. I didn't imagine it."

"And are you positive about it?"

"Yes I am."

"Thank you, my Lord. I have completed my questions of this witness."

A bewildered Bruce Drever was led from the witness stand. George Barr sat at his laptop, peering at the little screen. He tapped at the keyboard and examined the screen again. A corner of his mouth lifted into a kind of smile. The Honorary Sheriff, Charlie Sinclair, coughed.

"Mr Barr. Your next witness?"

He looked again at the laptop. Clicking, focussing on the screen. He smiled and rose.

"The defence wishes to call Inspector Roland Clett to the stand."

Clett looked questioningly at Sigurd Rostung, who raised his eyebrows. Clett swore to tell the truth and stood in the witness box. George Barr stood, slowly positioning himself in front of Clett.

"Inspector Clett, the defence council has just referred to the forensic report SPSA/144B/10. That purports to identify the blood on my client's sweatshirt as that of Geraldine Work."

"Yes," said Clett.

"Can you read the date from the report please?"

Clett took the report and read from the front page:

"The 13th June 2010."

"Thank you, Inspector."

Barr went to his table and lifted his laptop, returning to the witness box.

"Now Inspector, here on my laptop is a screen which shows the formal submission of that same forensic report, reference SPSA/144B/10. Do you agree?"

Clett examined the laptop screen.

"I agree."

"Would you please read out from my screen the date that the file was saved and electronically write-protected."

Clett felt his stomach lurch as he examined the file datestamp from the screen. He swallowed and read the date:

"The electronic date on the file is the 12th June 2010."

"I see; but the date on the printout is the thirteenth of June."

"Yes."

"My lord, as this document constitutes evidence that is harmful to my client, I submit that it is inadmissible due to this anomaly. How could the document be dated with a date after it was saved and write protected for submission?"

There was silence as people took in this information.

"Inspector, I would now like to consider the forensic report, reference SPSA/144C/10, in respect of the analysis of the bloodstain on the carpet of the Fraction nightclub. Once more, could you read the date on the printout?"

Clett held the report, trying to still his trembling hand. He cleared his throat:

"The 13th of June 2010."

"Again, thank you Inspector."

Once more, Barr offered Clett his laptop.

"Now Inspector, can you now read the electronic date stamp for the report reference SPSA/144C/10?"

"The 12th June 2010."

"Thank you for your assistance, Inspector."

Ronnie Rust clapped George Barr's back as he replaced the

laptop. The Honorary Sheriff Charlie Sinclair took his gavel and hit the block.

"The court will adjourn for consideration of this new information. We shall re-convene at 10.00 tomorrow morning."

* * *

Sigurd Rostung inhaled on his cigarette, paused, then blew the smoke out into the chill winter air. The snow had stopped, but a new white coating covered the spire of St Magnus' Cathedral, and the surrounding graveyard. Clett stood next to him as they surveyed the scene in front of them.

"This is a shambles, Sigurd. Rust is going to walk."

"Perhaps Roland, but alas, this is the cogs of justice at work. You just have to allow yourself be carried along with the flow."

"Aye, Sigurd. But what about that DNA evidence?"

"I fear it will fail. Most cases that fail are down to things like this, you know."

"I don't know how it could have happened."

"A clerical error. You know, not everything is ordered and predictable. We are but the playthings of the fates."

"I know, I know, I know, but Rust will get off."

Sigurd pulled his light court gown around his shoulders, ineffective against the cold, and exhaled into the chill air.

"Such snow in Orkney. Haven't seen it like this since I was a boy."

ice

T-Block, RAF Whale Head
Friday 20th November 1942

Henry sat across the transmitter room from Sergeant Jack Cameron. The transmitter hummed and gurgled and sucked as it transmitted its pulses to the aerial masts, creating a curtain of radio waves in the ether, protecting the country from the evil of the hun. The blue light shone out of the cabinet observation window and was reflected on the ceiling with an elliptical pool of dancing blue light. Henry took a fresh sheet of paper and wrote his address at the top of the page. Staring at it, he scribbled it out, scrunched up the paper and took another.

Dear Miss Hall,

> *Please allow me to introduce myself. My name is Henry Long. I work in T-Block and I have seen you many times in the NAAFI. You might have noticed me. I am the one who reads the technical journals. I am twenty-one years old and I have watched you for many months, and I have tried to speak to you, but I cannot speak and I become tongue tied. I tried, and I was too nervous. I am sorry. I listen to your voice on the r/t, and I feel I know you. I just know there is something between us, and I think that you know it too. I feel that the time has come for me to tell you that I have realised that I am in love with you. There. I*

have said it. I am in love with you. My father is a
coal merchant.

Well, that is all about me. I will now tell
you why I am writing you a letter. I have wanted
to write to you because…

Henry looked at the unfinished letter. They were honest words, but maybe he needed a different approach that would make her forget about the time in the canteen. Maybe more romantic? Yes, he would write her a poem. He tore up the letter, took a fresh sheet and wrote:

Dearest Charlotte, my love, my life
When you smile,
I lose myself in your smile
Your eyes are the colour of the sky
Your hair like the ocean wave.

And you? And you?
Your translucence, like the ether,
that shimmers in this northern light,
your aura that I perceive,
your aura that lights the dim;

And you? And you?
When will you see me?
This boy who will die for you
This boy who would kill for you.

Watergate Sheriff Court, Kirkwall
Friday 17th December 2010

The honorary Sheriff Charlie Sinclair tapped his block lightly.

"I have concluded that the DNA evidence submitted by the prosecution, reference SPSA/144B/10, and SPSA/144C/10 is not deemed admissible. I would advise the jury that they must disregard it. Mr Barr, do you wish to continue?"

"Indeed, I do, my Lord."

George Barr, Writer to the Signet, took the floor once more.

"Ladies and gentlemen, you have heard this morning from my

learned friend who has presented for the prosecution. I have to tell you that in the interests of clarity and justice, we will continue to contest every detail of that case."

He turned to Rust and nodded.

"Many people on these islands know, and, I would suggest, love my client. Mister Rust is a local man who has engaged in a number of good works for this community."

A murmur of approval came from the gallery. Sigurd Rostung stood.

"Objection, my Lord. This has no bearing on the matter of the case."

The Honorary Sheriff Charlie Sinclair addressed Rust's lawyer.

"Mr Barr, this is not a popularity contest. Please move on."

Barr brushed some cigarette ash from his gown.

"My Lord, I was merely attempting to demonstrate the qualities, if you will, the virtuous character of my client."

"Move on, Mr Barr."

"Certainly, my Lord."

Barr put his hands in his pockets as he paced in front of the witness box.

"Ladies and gentlemen of the jury, all that is left of the prosecution's case is the testimony of the arresting officer Inspector Roland Clett. I would like to recall Inspector Clett to the witness stand."

Clett came forward.

"Inspector, I would remind you that you are still under oath."

Clett tried to speak but found his mouth dry. He coughed: "I understand." He clenched and unclenched his fists, but the shaking continued; steadying himself, gripping the small shelf below the level of the witness stand; slowing his breathing.

"Inspector Clett, how long have you been an Inspector in the Northern Constabulary?"

"Since 21st April 2010."

"About eight months. Indeed, were you not promoted on the day of the murder of Dominic Byrd at Noup Head?"

"Yes."

"What was your position before that?"

"I was in Strathclyde division."

"In what capacity?"

"I was a sergeant, seconded to the Scottish Crime and Drug Enforcement Agency."

"Why did you leave Strathclyde?"

Sigurd Rostung stood to his feet.

"My Lord, Objection. This is a matter of record. It has no bearing on the case at hand."

"I tend to agree. Please move on, Mr Barr."

"Certainly, my Lord, I merely wish to ascertain the level of experience and competence of the officer giving witness."

"That is not in question, Mr Barr."

"With the greatest of respect, I submit that the competence of this officer is very much in question."

"Mr Barr, I will allow you to continue, but you had better prove your point. I will not allow the haranguing of a police officer for no reason."

"Thank you, my Lord. Inspector Clett, is it not true that you left Strathclyde division because of a botched operation that resulted in the death of a young man that was down to your incompetence?"

Clett's vision was swimming. He was breathing in short gulps.

"I disagree. The subsequent investigation did not find my activities in any way unusual; the verdict of the inquiry was death by misadventure."

"So you say. Moving on to your relationship with Mister Rust, how long have you known him?"

"I have known your client since we were boys. We were at the same school."

"You were friends?"

"We were not friends."

"Enemies then?"

"I have nothing in common with the defendant."

"So you say, but you can surely not deny, Inspector, that you have an irrational hatred of my client; that you have hounded him for years? Indeed, is it not the case that that now you see an opportunity to punish him for some perceived unknown misdeed of the past?"

"I have…"

"Please let me finish, Inspector. Did you or did you not arrest my client on a previous occasion – an arrest that was entirely unjustified, where   my   client   was   totally   exonerated?" Sigurd Rostung rose to his feet.

"Objection, my Lord. This is outrageous. My learned colleague cannot bring up this subject."

The Honorary Sheriff nodded

"I agree. Mister Barr. Withdraw your question."

"As my Lordship wishes."

Clett coughed. He took a deep breath. "My Lord, I do not mind responding."

"As you wish, Inspector."

"That arrest was in relation to an assault at sea. The case satisfied the Procurator Fiscal. Subsequently, the defendant was found not guilty in court. This is not the same thing as an unjustified arrest, as you should know, Mr Barr."

"Quite, quite; let's just move on, shall we? So, Inspector Clett, how would you describe your relationship with my client?"

"As I have said, I do not have a relationship with the defendant."

"Oh come on, Inspector. This man has been your bête noire for years. While you have had a plodding career beset by failure, my client has grown in stature in the community from the most humble of origins. I would go as far as to say that he has gained respect and love on these islands. I submit that you do have an antipathy towards my client. This is what has motivated you to make this arrest. Your intention was to bring him down in the public eye by means of this charge today."

"Absolutely not. I have no opinion about this man. My motivations are professional."

"I think the jury will see your motivations for what they are, Inspector. I would now like to move on to the arrest that led to my client's presence here today. At around eight-fifteen pm, on Tuesday twenty-seventh of April 2010, you went to the home of my client in Olfsquoy Crescent, Kirkwall. There you arrested him."

"That is correct."

"Did you caution him?"

"I did."

"Can verify this?"

"Sorry?"

"Did you record the arrest in your notebook?"

Clett held tight on to the front of the witness box, his knuckles white.

"No, but…"

"Did you have a second police officer present?"

"No. The defendant was cautioned at Burgh Road Police station in the presence of other officers. Normal procedures were followed."

"Perhaps so, but isn't it a fundamental tenet in police training that everything is recorded in an officer's notebook?"

"Correct procedures were followed."

"I see. Thank you, Inspector. Let's move on, shall we? Can you tell me if you are taking any medication?"

Sigurd Rostung stood.

"Objection my Lord. This can have no bearing on this case. Surely…"

Clett interrupted.

"My Lord, I have no objection to answering that question."

"If you are sure, Inspector Clett. You are not on trial here."

"Thank you, my Lord. I have nothing to hide. I am not on any medication."

"But you have been on medication, Inspector, haven't you? I put it to the court that this officer is experiencing further mental health difficulties and his motivation against my client is driven by irrational paranoia."

Sigurd Rostung took to his feet.

"Objection, my Lord. This is preposterous."

"Sustained. Mr Barr, that is enough. Are there any more questions?"

"No more questions my Lord."

Clett stumbled as he stood down from the stand, gripping the handrail for security as the Sheriff Clerk announced:

"The court shall adjourn until two o'clock."

* * *

George Barr blew his nose and stuffed the handkerchief back in his pocket.

"My Lord, I would wish to call to the stand, the defendant, Mister Ronald Gerald Rust."

Ronnie Rust rose and ambled across the floor to the witness box. He smiled broadly as he took the oath.

"Mister Rust, you are the owner of the Fraction Nightclub?"

"I do indeed have that pleasure."

"Thank you. Do you own this car?"

Barr showed a picture of a silver BMW, licence number RUS5.

"I do. It is one of two cars I own. The other is RUS6."

George Barr gave the picture to the clerk who handed it to the jury.

"I should like to refer to the sweatshirt used in evidence by the prosecution."

The clerk held up the item in a shrink-wrapped bag. Barr handed it to Rust.

"Mister Rust, is this your sweatshirt?"

"Eh, yes, it is."

"Indeed, you wore it on the night of the assault on Miss Geraldine Work."

"Yes, that poor girl. You do know, don't you, that I couldn't harm a hair on that girl's head? She was my right arm at Fraction – couldn't have run the place without her."

"Thank you. Shall we return to the bloodstained item of clothing?"

"Anything I can do to help the court."

"The staining on the sweatshirt is human blood, type O, the same blood type as Geraldine Work."

"Yes. It is also my own blood type, so I have been told."

Barr turned towards the Honorary Sheriff.

"My Lord, I would now like to refer to the forensic report on this sweatshirt, reference SPSA/144B/10 dated the 13th June 2010."

"Mr Barr, following your own submission, and due to the date anomalies, I have already deliberated that this evidence is inadmissible."

"I thank Your Lordship, but I would like to clarify this matter for the benefit of the members of the jury in the interest of openness and justice."

"Please be brief."

"As your Lordship wishes."

Barr gave a copy to Rust, who thumbed through it.

"This report, although incorrectly dated, and previously deemed inadmissible, states that this blood was type O positive. This is Ms Geraldine Work's blood type. Coincidentally, it is also the blood type of the defendant."

The court murmured while Rust shook his head, smiling.

"Mister Rust, you smile. Do you find these proceedings amusing?"

"No, sir, I do not. I was thinking on how my sweatshirt became so stained."

"Please tell the court."

"I had a nosebleed."

A snigger came from the public gallery. Rust grinned; Sinclair tapped the gavel on the block in irritation.

"Order, order."

Barr put both his hands in his pockets.

"Mister Rust let me be clear. You are asking the court to believe that you had a nosebleed?"

"Yes, I get them a lot. What a mess it makes. Quite embarrassing, really."

"Mister Rust, what do you say about this forensic report that states clearly that this blood is from your nightclub manager, Miss Geraldine Work?"

"I'm sorry, but I don't know where that's coming from. Your chaps must have made a mistake, some kind of mix-up. It was a simple nosebleed. That's all. Sorry about that, it was just a nosebleed; after all the trouble your chaps have gone to. Sorry."

Clett shook his head. Barr continued:

"Mister Rust. I would like now to present to you the second Forensic report, reference SPSA/144B/10, also incorrectly dated 13th June 2010."

Rust flicked through the three-page report and put it to the side.

"Mister Rust, this report concerns a further analysis of blood stains from the carpet of the Fraction Nightclub, in the lounge. Do you recognise the location from the photograph on page two?"

"I do."

"Once more, this report identifies the blood type as type O, that of Geraldine Work."

"And mine."

"And yours. The analysis also claims that the blood is from Miss Geraldine Work. What can you say about this? Another nosebleed?"

"Yes."

"Can you expand, please?"

"Certainly. I had the nosebleed in the nightclub. I felt so embarrassed; Geraldine had just finished cleaning up, but there I was pouring blood all over her nice clean carpet. She was great about it though. Told me to go home to clean myself up; that she would tidy the place after I'd gone. That girl is an absolute gem, you know."

"But, to return to the forensic report, Mister Rust, it categorically identifies this blood sample as that of Geraldine Work."

"I am terribly sorry, but I'm afraid that your chaps have cocked up here too. It really was just a nosebleed. I'm awfully sorry I've created all this trouble over such a silly little thing."

"So you deny that the blood on your sweatshirt, and on the floor of the Fraction nightclub is that of Geraldine Work; you deny the evidence in these reports?"

"I'm so sorry, but yes."

* * *

Clett stood on the steps of Kirkwall Sheriff Court, on Watergate, in the shadow of the spire of St Magnus Cathedral. Snow had turned to slush around the door to the court, but out over the grassy surroundings it lay as far as he could see. The noise of the town was absorbed by the recent fall, the whole world seeming clear in this moment; unlike the whirlwind of thoughts circulating in Clett's mind. He breathed slowly, sucking in the cold air, replenishing himself for another humiliating session. His phone buzzed.

"Inspector, Norman here. How did it go this morning?"

"Not good, Norman. Terrible, in fact; but never mind all that, what do you have?"

"About 'The Count': no progress on identification, but we visited the site with Sanja and Irene. We found a sick sheep. It had ingested a plastic bag and guess what?"

"The bag had traces of Ether."

"Spot on, sir!"

"Thanks Norman. At last, progress. That explains that. So; suicide with complications; who put the bread and this grey powder on the body? The Polish tourist, Jerzy Przybylski, is still not to be discounted. I think we should bring him in for questioning. Whose idea was it to look at the sheep?"

"I couldn't possibly say."

"You're a clever man, Norman Clouston."

As Clett ended the call, Geraldine Work stumbled up the stairs of the Sheriff Court, using a stick for support.

"Geraldine, where have you been?"

"Sorry Inspector, I was at wee Raymond's Children's Hearing. They placed him with his Nan on Shapinsay. I'm not allowed to see him, but that's better than him staying in a home, or with strangers, isn't it? And, do you know, it's all down to Mister Rust."

"What?"

"He spoke up for me; you know, made a few phone calls. He would have been at the hearing, but he was otherwise engaged. Such a busy man; He is an absolute saint."

"But, Geraldine, you do know you are to give evidence against him today?"

"I know, but it will all turn out right in the end. Mister Rust says so."

"You've spoken to him?"

"I, eh…"

They entered the courtroom and sat in the public gallery. Geraldine using the stick for support, still trembling. Clett bent to whisper to Sigurd Rostung, whose expression lost any indication of animation. George Barr took the floor.

"I would like to recall Mr Ronald Rust to the stand."

Rust smiled at the jury and winked at Geraldine.

"Mister Rust, can you describe your reaction to the assault on Ms Geraldine Work?"

"Ladies and gentlemen of the jury, I have to say how profoundly sorry I was to hear of this assault; awful, just awful. I have tried to help the police with their enquiries, but they have as yet been unable to find the assailant. Miss Work has been known to me for several years; it was myself that gave her employment at a time she needed to regain some self-respect. It is not surprising she has not been able to testify today; I can understand how frightened she must be of a reprisal."

Sigurd Rostung stood.

"Objection, my Lord. This is not a platform for the defendant. He must answer the question."

"I agree, Mr Rostung. Answer the question, Mister Rust."

Rust smiled again at Geraldine Work, who looked to the floor, crying silently, with a nervous, quivering smile.

"It is just a terrible thing to have happened on these beautiful islands we call home."

"Thank you, Mister Rust. Now I would like you to describe your relationship with Inspector Clett."

"Well, Mr Barr, I consider myself something of an expert in the field of human nature…"

"Objection my Lord," Sigurd Rostung drawled from the prosecution bench, rising to his feet.

The Honorary Sheriff looked towards Rust:

"Please answer the question, Mister Rust."

"I apologise, my Lord. Roland and I; yes, I never really thought of us as friends exactly, more acquaintances, on good nodding terms if you will. We were together at school and I always supported his career. I will admit to having put in the odd word for him that I feel must have helped in some little way. But, you know, I don't know. Roland has a weak side and, you know, he possibly has been privately a little bitter about my success; perhaps this bitterness might have grown despite my attempts to help him. Maybe I could have done more, but it seems to me that it is this has brought us here today."

In the gallery, Clett clenched his teeth. Their eyes met as Rust continued, pleasantly:

"I feel no animosity towards Roland; in spite of all this unpleasantness, I will continue to help in any way I can, but I think it is important to realise where this accusation has come from."

"Thank you, Mister Rust. That will be all from the defence, my Lord."

The Honorary Sheriff Charlie Sinclair lazily tapped his gavel on the block.

"Thank you, Mr Barr. Mr Rostung, do you have anything else?"

"Thank you, my Lord. Miss Work is now present. If it please the court, I would like to call her as a witness."

"Once again, with the very generous latitude of the defence."

The Honorary Sheriff nodded to Barr and Rust. Rust waved at Barr, who responded: "No objection my lord."

"I will allow this."

Geraldine stepped into the witness box and mumbled the oath. Her gaze fixed on her feet. Rostung came close to the witness box.

"Geraldine; may I call you Geraldine?"

"Yes, if you like."

"Ok Geraldine. At the time of the assault, you were the

manager of the Fraction Nightclub, owned by the accused, Ronald Gerald Rust?"

"Yes. Mister Rust has been very good to me."

"I see; can you describe the events of the afternoon of the twenty-seventh of April, this year?"

"It was like Mister Rust said. I was doing a stock check in the nightclub and he had a nosebleed, all over the carpet. Poor man, he was so embarrassed."

There was a collective intake of breath around the courtroom. Clett sat bolt upright. Rostung raised his eyebrows.

"Just a minute, Miss Work. The allegation is that Ronald Rust assaulted you, indeed that he assaulted you so severely that you required hospitalisation. May I remind you that you are under oath?"

"That's what happened."

"So, can you tell the court why you were in hospital?"

"Oh, it was nothing really, I just fell."

"Miss Work, you had such severe injuries that you could not have received them by a mere fall. Miss Work, I put it to you that you were assaulted by the defendant to such an extent that your life was in danger. You said so in your statement."

"No, it wasn't like that, at all."

"Miss Work. I cannot understand your testimony today. It contradicts in every way your signed statement to the police."

"I was very upset when I said all that stuff. I wasn't myself."

Sigurd Rostung shook his head and turned to face the Sheriff, shrugging his shoulders. He turned again to Geraldine.

"Miss Work, have you been in communication with the defendant prior to this court attendance?"

"Well, sort of. Yes. He helped me so much with my wee Raymond."

"Can you tell the court if he told you what to say today?"

"Not really, he just made a few phone calls, you know; he put in a word for me with the Children's Panel to stop Raymond going into care."

"Did he really?"

George Barr took to his feet.

"Objection, my Lord. If this young woman has spoken to my client, this testimony is tainted and unreliable."

"I agree Mr Barr. Young woman, have you communicated with

the defendant, Ronald Rust prior to this trial?"

"Mister Rust, well, er, yes; that is, I telephoned him."

"How many times?"

"I don't know, really. A few times, I suppose. He was helping me."

"Miss Work, you have wasted this court's time. Indeed, I will be considering whether you should be charged with contempt. Enough of this. Case dismissed!"

The Honorary Sheriff Charlie Sinclair hit the block rather harder than was his manner. The gavel clipped its side and came in contact with the bench; the sound shrill and thin.

* * *

Ronnie Rust stepped out on to the brown slush outside Sheriff Court with George Barr, into the freezing Kirkwall drizzle, to be met by several reporters including Janie Shearer.

"Mister Rust, how do you feel about your acquittal?"

"Hello Janie, nice to see you here." He winked, and she blushed.

"I have to say that I feel vindicated. The scurrilous lies and insinuations that have been made against me once more by certain individuals in the Orkney Police department have again been proved to be such in a court of law."

"Will you be seeking compensation?"

"No Janie, I will not waste public money. I have been found innocent in a court of law. That is good enough for me."

"Mister Rust, what are your plans now?"

"I intend to continue to devote my life to this community, and to the eradication of corruption in the police system. To allow me to pursue this path alongside my other community pursuits, I can now announce that I will be standing as a councillor in the coming local elections."

"Mister Rust..."

Inside the court, Geraldine Work sat in the public gallery.

"I'm sorry, Inspector. I did it for wee Raymond."

* * *

Clett removed a crumpled photocopy from his pocket and stared at it, mechanically, not really reading it:

> *To Mr Murdoch Mackenzie,*
> *Kirkwall High School,*
>
> *December 20th 1746*
> *Dear Mr Mackenzie,*
> *Sir, I have to tell you that you are a power for genius. Ice. Of course. You must lay your Iron chain upon the ice – the perfect medium for your meridian. Ha Ha! I have heard that the Loch of Kirbuster, by Germiston, is a shallow body of water that has been seen to ice up fully in a hard frost. It is on higher ground and so is more likely to freeze. With the cold winter ahead of us, we may have an opportunity to mark out your meridian.*
>
> *I shall await your company at Mrs Eunson's on Monday.*
> *Arch'd Clett of Canmore*

CHAPTER EIGHT

gasoline

Houton Ferry to Lyness
Sunday 22nd November 1942

Charlotte Hall showed her twelve-fifty pass to the guard at the Houton ferry. The sky above Scapa Flow was filled with barrage balloons tethered to any piece of available land, and to trawlers moored in the flow. Among the seaplanes, the little ferry weaved its way to the jetty. Charlotte was in a state of excited exhaustion. She had taken ten hours to travel from Whale Head, by way of Kettletoft, the ferry to Kirkwall, the bus to Houton, and now another ferry to Lyness. Lyness; the nearest thing to London Society on offer in Orkney.

Charlotte stood on the quay, avoiding the mud as a half-track rumbled past. A seaplane splashed down in its unusual elegance and sailed to a berth across the harbour. Charlotte thought of Mergret Isbister, and her efforts to maintain ownership of her fate by destroying her paintings, to achieve some element of control over this mad world. She took out her lighter and ran her thumb over the inscription:

> *For Charlotte,*
> *with all my love,*
> *your Jim.*

She re-read the letter she had kept for weeks. Would he still turn up? In this war, any notion between two people of planning to meet at a particular time and place was faintly ridiculous. What with the inconsistencies of travel, the need to follow orders that might take one to the other end of the country with little notice: who knew, Jim might not arrive for another week, or he could be posted elsewhere. They had arranged that they should meet when his ship came in at Scapa, and Charlotte had received the telegram with their private code; all she knew was that Jim was arriving in Orkney, and to meet at the NAAFI Theatre in Lyness.

Charlotte found the women's accommodation block, where she met her chum, Andie, an old girlfriend from training, who had access to a bath. They did each other's hair, and shared lipstick and spoke of their old life, of school days, back home in the warm predictable south. When she was finished, she studied herself in the mirror. After fifteen months at Whale Head, her skin had roughened with the wind, but a bit of rouge worked wonders. Her new uniform was a better fit; she knew Jim would like how she looked.

Charlotte and Andie made their way to the NAAFI theatre. It was huge, unlike the little NAAFI in Whale Head. Hundreds of service men and women milled around, laughing, anticipating the dancing to come.

Then, in the sea of forces uniforms, she saw Jim, and he saw her. Amongst the chaos and confusion all around, they had found each other.

"Here you are, Jim Manners, here you are," said Charlotte.

"Yes, darling. Here we are."

They said little and gazed at each other, still in disbelief that the person opposite was really there, present, close, together, in this dance hall, in this war, despite the upset and disruption that engaged the whole world.

The five-piece RAF Band started up, and in seconds the crowd took to the floor as one. Charlotte and Jim danced, each mirroring the other's movements, their bodies melding into a single fluid form, flowing in the throng, swaying to the music.

They bought beer and lemonade and danced some more. Charlotte looked at her watch.

"The last ferry leaves in fifteen minutes."

Charlotte touched Jim's hand.

"I don't want to leave."

"Don't."

"Where will I sleep?"

"I know somewhere. I have a car. It's just an old jalopy."

"What about petrol?"

"I've been saving coupons."

Jim hugged Charlotte, tight. "Oh I do love you. You are wonderful. In these terrible times, you are my love."

The RAF Band played Chatanooga-choo-choo as Charlotte and Jim waved to Andie who was dancing wildly. They went out into the Orkney night, shivered and held each other close.

"Gosh, an open-top car in Orkney in December. Jim Manners, you must be mad."

"It's a Riley Nine. She's a corker. Here's a blanket."

Charlotte tied a headscarf under her chin.

"That's hardly going to keep you warm!"

"If I'm having a ride in an open-topped Riley, I'm going to look like Bette Davis."

In the cold night, Jim and Charlotte drove south, out of Lyness. Their breath, exhaled out into the frosty air, created little clouds. Stars shone through the gaps between the blimps, the barrage balloons that populated the sky, that protected Charlotte and Jim in the Riley, rolling softly along on the single-track road.

"Those blimps; it is as if they are supporting the weight of the whole of Orkney. They keep us afloat, making us safe from the bombs."

Jim brushed Charlotte's knee as he double de-clutched to change down for a corner. She smiled, keeping her eyes ahead, the dull slit of their headlights illuminating the few feet ahead of them. The little car cruised silently, floating between the road and the intermittent stars, this little time of love and joy between discomfort and uncertainty. Their shoulders rubbed with each little bump, and they shared their warmth in the freezing night. They breathed the cold air that nipped their nostrils, their breath rising into the sky, dissolving in the vapours of the night.

"I wonder... if the blimps weren't there, the islands might sink into the sea. Just a pair of scissors would do it, you know, snip snip."

Jim put his hand over Charlotte's. "I think you'd need more than a pair of scissors to cut through those hawsers."

"Oh, I don't know. They say that sometimes they come adrift from their moorings."

"And do the islands sink a little when a blimp becomes free?"

"Don't be silly, Jim, darling. You would have to cut away all the balloons for there to be any danger of us falling into the sea."

Out to their left, in the silhouetted ships on Scapa Flow, in the soft rumble of idling ships' engines, they saw flashes and sparks from a welder on one of the ships.

"Someone will be on a fizzer for that. You will be able to see that for miles. You might as well say 'come and bomb us, Jerry'."

Charlotte leaned over and kissed him on the cheek.

"Jim. Settle down. It's just you and me here, now."

The Riley floated on the road, winding south, until they stopped at an old Martello Tower. To the north and east, over the whole Flow, the swarm of blimps dotted the night sky, the canopy of night beyond. Jim turned off the engine, and there was silence, with only distant thumps and the odd hammering far off.

"What is this place?"

"Hackness. It's a gun emplacement, built in Napoleonic times; walls are eight-feet thick. The chap in charge owes me a favour." When they approached, the guard raised his rifle.

"Who goes there?"

Jim responded: "Charlie, isn't it? The watchword is Panacea, and Sergeant Smith is expecting us."

The young guard grinned sheepishly, trying not to stare at Charlotte. She was different alright. Charlotte smiled, and he blushed.

"Aye, sir. You're expected. Go on up."

Jim led Charlotte up the steel steps to the entrance, into the warm thick stone enclosure.

"Where are we going?"

He kissed her on the cheek.

"Wait and see."

He led them down stairs to a windowless cubicle. As they descended into the stone structure, they felt the heat rising to meet them.

"Just a minute."

Jim lit a match and used it to light a dozen candle-stubs around the chamber. In the dim light, Charlotte saw a fire bucket with a bottle of champagne and two tin mugs at the side of a camp bed.

"Jim, you devil."

They kissed, then poured the champagne, toasting their happiness.

"Oh Charlotte, I am so glad you are here. Gosh! This is not what I'd imagined, but it is so wonderful, isn't it?"

In their unfamiliarity with intimacy, they bumped noses and their arms got in each other's way; and, slowly, their clumsiness turned to softness as they became more sure of themselves, more trusting of the other's movements, of the other's body. They sat on the camp bed, pulling gently at their clothes. Jim struggled with Charlotte's underwear, and she helped, smiling shyly. They lay down, giggling on the narrow flimsy bed; Charlotte scraped her knee on the rough canvas. As they rolled on top of each other, the bed collapsed under them. There was a moment's silence, and they roared in laughter, lying on top of what was left of the camp bed.

"What were you thinking, Jim, darling?"

"I know, old girl. I was never one for the practicalities of life."

"And they put you in charge of men?"

"Well, the chaps look after me, really."

They drank some more champagne and moved the thin mattress and covers nearer to the stove.

Finstown
Friday 17th December 2010

The Clett's home was a traditional pebble-dashed bungalow like many other homes on the islands, built low to avoid the wind. It had a short drive to a garage that was never used, filled with odds and ends: a canoe from when the family thought they would go kayaking every year, an old tent, ladders, pots of paint, golf clubs, outdoor furniture, a barbecue, and a lawn mower. In the middle of the garden was the head of a standing stone sticking out over the snow-covered grass. Four upright pillars of rough granite marked the boundary of the garden. Beneath the snow, patterns in the grass had been made by regular mowing, creating patches that appeared now as little white mounds. Above the green front door, a bamboo wind-chime sounded a woody peal in the breeze. The house just in sight of Wideforde Hill, covered in snow, its radio masts piercing the grey sky.

Clett sat at his desk, surrounded by various piles of photocopies and printouts scattered around the small, study. With a swipe of his arm, he swept all the papers and books to the floor.

He felt a touch on his shoulder.

"Sorry, I didn't hear you."

Clett looked out to the garden, to the rowan. The rowan was made up of three intertwined trunks, the trunks pleated when they were soft and pliant. A rock been had placed in the gap in the middle of the entwined trunks and fused with the tree, embracing it in its rings.

Birds were eating seeds left out earlier by Christine.

"Christine, I, I eh…"

He took a deep breath.

"Rust's lawyer saw right through me."

"He understood everything; how much I hate Rust, how it has affected my objectivity. I am a laughing stock at the office."

"Roland, that's not true."

"It's not the first time. Clouston shut down an email when I approached his desk."

"Roland, listen to yourself."

"It had my name on it."

"That means nothing."

"They are all in on it, even young Keldie. What am I going to do? I can't afford another six months off work."

Christine put her hand on his.

"You know this is irrational, don't you?"

He gazed out of the window.

"Roland. This is not real. Tell me that you see that this is not real."

Outside, two crows fought over a fatball, scattering seeds on the snow.

Clett picked up a photocopy from the floor.

To Mr Murdoch Mackenzie,
Kirkwall High School,
December 20th 1744

Dear Mr Mackenzie,
I am happy that you have established your
meridian here on our Orkney Islands. To
achieve a chained line of three miles and
a quarter with lines and ropes and chain
on the ice. I ken that your Loch of
Stannous is a better choice as it offers a
longer run over the ice. What work, what
toil   to   your   newe   science   of
Hydrographie.

I fear I may not attend at Mrs
Eunson's on Monday. I must go for a
funeral of my old neighbour John Sinclair

> *of Gyre. He was a wise man. You should*
> *have met him.*
> > *Yrs. &C.*
> > *Arch'd Clett of Canmore*

Sent today at 11:02:03
From: Irene Seath
Subject: ORK/2010/12/14/Lopness SPSA SOCO
Preliminary observations
To: Roland Clett (Insp); Margaret McPhee (CI)
Cc: Norman Clouston (Sgt); Sanja Dilpit (SOCO)
Good morning Inspector. Salient extracts from ORK/2010/12/14/Lopness (Full report on secure drive):
Para 3.13:
"Noted prominent organ congestion; a remarkable pulmonary oedema. Toxicological analysis of the blood by head-space chromatography revealed presence of diethyl ether, at a concentration of 127.7 mg/d. Histopathological examination of the lungs showed a picture of the oedema and prominent congestion. There is an absence of any significant recent drug or alcohol deposit, but relevant examination of the liver showed congestion of a medium degree."
Para 5.2
"It would appear that the deceased had poured the ether on a handkerchief and placed it inside the plastic bag before putting it over his head. No known history of ether or other substance abuse. No suicide note has yet been found. Concentration of ether in the blood (127.7 mg/dl) is within the concentrations achieved during surgical anaesthesia (50-150 mg/dl) and close to the average concentration for deep surgical anaesthesia (120 mg/dl). This leads us to the conclusion that the death was due to asphyxiation rather than an anaesthetic type death. However, this distinction can be regarded as irrelevant to the outcome. The person would have been unconscious during the asphyxiation. Subject to the coroner's deliberation, it is anticipated that the death may be classified as suicide."

Para 6

"The body was found with a small dish containing bread and a grey powder. this powder was found to be a primitive unrefined form of **Na Cl** -Sodium Chloride. The colouration might indicate contaminants that may help identify a specific source. A sample has been sent for isotopic analysis. Results will be communicated when available."

Para 7.3

"A small pebble was found inside the left shoe of the deceased. His left foot was calloused, and on the upper torso a rash was observed. Horse hair fibres were found in this area stuck to his skin. Many of the fibres had punctured the skin, leaving wounds that appeared to have been seeping blood at a low level for a very long period of time. Scarring indicates that this irritation had been experienced by the individual for decades."

Once again, another update tomorrow at 11.00 as per SPSA SLA (2008). As always, please get in touch if any queries arise.

Regards

Sanja Dilpit. (SOCO) 07222 176688

Irene Seath (SOCO) 07222 176687

Finstown
Saturday 18th December 2.30 am

Ronnie Rust switched off his headlights as he turned south off the Main Street on the quarry road, parking opposite the Clett's bungalow. His watch read one-thirty. The only sounds were of his steps on the crunching snow as he walked across to the house, tried the front door, went around the side, past the green Polo and red Mazda, and entered by the back door. As his eyes became accustomed to the dark, he put the kettle on, and sat at the kitchen table while the water boiled. He found teabags, took milk from the fridge and chose a mug that said 'Yosemite', all the while scanning photos of the Clett family, a calendar, the shopping list on a whiteboard: *tin toms, cappuccino, eggs, milk...*

Rust moved to the sitting room, lifting things at random. Selecting an ornate Russian doll, a matryoshka, he dismantled it, lining up the nested dolls in order. Tossing a cushion to the floor, he sat in an armchair, placing the mug on the coffee table, next to a circular mat, listening to the soft snoring upstairs, the ticking of a clock, the sound of two oystercatchers in conversation in the garden. He switched on the television, turning the volume down as he flicked through the channels. He stopped at a Second World War documentary. Hitler was gesticulating to a crowd, spraying silent spittle from his mouth. Rust took the smallest matryoska, examined it, and put it in his pocket. He re-assembled the remaining dolls, putting them back on the sideboard.

Rust brought the mug of tea upstairs to the study. A computer sat in the middle of the untidy desk in the moonlight, its little light flashing red. He moved the mouse, and the screen came alive with a background of the Clett family at a barbecue somewhere. It waited for a password. Rust examined the items on the wall: the postcards, even more family photos, photocopies of ancient documents. Nothing about work. Out the window, in the moonlight, he saw the old gnarled rowan tree with entwined trunks. He took a last gulp of the tea and placed the cup on the desk, spun away from the study, opened the bedroom door and paused, listening to the quiet rumble of snoring. Rust went into the bathroom, lifted the toilet seat, and urinated into the pan, splashing on the floor as he looked around. He entered the bedroom, went to the dressing table, took Christine's hairbrush, and picked some hairs from it. He took a bottle of perfume and sniffed. Rust examined a pair of earrings and put one in his pocket, replacing the other on the dresser. Then he stepped across the room and stood over Christine. She grunted and turned over. A strand of hair lay on her face and she tried to blow it away, then to move it with her hand. Rust lifted the hair from her cheek.

"Thank you," she mumbled. Rust touched her bare shoulder with a forefinger. Next to her, Clett was lying on his back, snoring softly. Rust looked out to his BMW parked across the road. Christine's clothes lay on a chair, still warm. He buried his face in them, and breathed deeply, twice. Feeling their soft texture between his fingers, he took a pair of her knickers, folded them, and put them in his pocket. Placing the little bundle of clothes back on the chair, he left the couple, went down the stairs, out of the front door, crossed the street to his car and drove off, revving the engine.

"What was that?" murmured Christine. Clett grunted and turned over.

CHAPTER NINE

nicotine

NAAFI, RAF Whale Head
Wednesday 25th November 1942

Henry pushed open the heavy blast door of the NAAFI canteen and saw Charlotte, back from her leave, sitting with a group of girls. As he entered, they whispered to each other, casting glances towards him. His cheeks flushed; she would have seen his poem when she returned, perhaps only today. Had she shown it to anyone else? He could never have imagined that she would let him down like that. Henry poured a cup of tea from the urn and brought it to his table, away from the radio that was tuned to the British Home Service, quietly announcing ways to cook meagre food. He sat at a table, opened his *Wireless World* and became aware of the quiet. There were twelve people in the NAAFI, three girls around Charlotte, and the rest, other officers, operators, other ranks. No one spoke. Henry grew uncomfortable. He was sure they were looking at him. He shuffled, turning the pages of his magazine, not seeing the words. It was as if the whole room was breathing together, breathing over him. Sergeant Jack Cameron came in and smiled at Charlotte, who turned her head in Henry's direction. Cameron nodded back and approached Henry's table.

"Private Long. May I join you?"

Henry glanced around him. Everyone was watching. He mumbled a response.

"Your Christian name is Henry, isn't it?"

Henry looked up to the dim light bulb that illuminated the NAAFI tearoom. The BBC Home Service emitted the peals of Big Ben sounding one o'clock. He answered through gritted teeth.

"Yes sir."

"Call me Jack."

Henry grunted. Cameron opened a pack of Camels, offering one.

"You know, Henry, girls are odd."

Henry accepted a cigarette and faced away from Cameron. The Canadian leaned close and spoke softly.

"Take Miss Hall, for example."

Henry ground his teeth. The sound of this man's voice polluted her name. He clenched his hands into fists.

"She's beautiful, isn't she?"

He put the Camels back into his pocket and took out a pipe, tapping it on the side of an ashtray. He filled the bowl with fresh tobacco from a leather pouch. Henry watched the officer's little operation but remained unresponsive. He placed the fat American cigarette between his lips. Jack Cameron took a book of matches, tore one off and struck it, offering the flame to Henry. Henry inhaled the different flavour, coughed, and raised his eyebrows.

"It's the Turkish they put in them."

Cameron's pipe rattled as he sucked, lighting the dry tobacco. When he was satisfied that it was glowing properly, he removed the pipe from his mouth, pointing it towards Henry.

"You have to appreciate that a girl like Charlotte, well she...how can I say, she...you know it's different for girls, and more so for a girl like her."

Henry coughed once more on the sharp tobacco; Cameron smiled.

"You know, there are lots of other girls who would appreciate your intelligence."

"Condescending prig," thought Henry.

"What about one of the local girls? You know, I hope you don't mind me saying this Henry. You are a nice boy; I wouldn't want your feelings to be hurt."

Henry allowed the lit tip of the cigarette to smoulder close, letting the red heat singe the little hairs on his fingers. He knew then how much he hated this man. He said nothing, but inwardly exploded. In his head he was working out a plan. It was becoming clear; he knew now that he would have to deal with the man sitting across the table, sucking noisily on his pipe.

The Kirkwall Hotel, Harbour Street
Saturday 18th December 2010

In the bar, Sanja was reading, and Irene was knitting, her needles clicking softly.

"Whit's the book?"

"Jane Eyre."

"Again? Ye've read that book a dozen times. Jist watch the film."

"Nae chance. Whit ur ye knittin'?"

"A wee jumper fur ma nephew."

"Looks nice. Complicated. How dae ye get that coloured pattern fae the wan ball o' wool?"

"It's the yarn, its multicoloured and the design just creates itsel' as ye knit. Look, here's the pattern, see how easy it is."

"Looks like chess instructions tae me."

"Naw, it's a' logical. A simple cipher with a rational outcome. Seein' a pattern come oot oan a pair of needles, from a wee row of loops, seein' it grow to become somethin' ye c'n wear, is brilliant. Perfect zen, really. How's yer man, anyway? Has his wife – whit's her name, Betty? – has she burnt his hoose doon yet?"

"Bertha – jist comin' tae that bit."

"Aye. Ah always thought she was the interestin' wan."

"Ye wantin' a gin?"

"Naw cranberry juice fur me."

"Keepin' yer urinary tract happy, dear?"

"Away back tae yer knittin', hen."

Irene's phone buzzed. She glanced at the screen.

"It's jist the Inspector acknowledging wur last report."

Near the Stennes Road
Saturday 18th December 2010

Clett drove west out of Kirkwall, past the now-white hump of Maes Howe. Out of the corner of his eye, he saw a group of vehicles parked at the Stones of Stenness. He turned right, up the Skaill road, stopping at the lay-by that served as a car park. A man wearing sunglasses, accompanied by an athletic woman, both of them wearing black suits, stood by two large black SUVs. One waved him on, but Clett drew in, winding down his window. The woman approached and gesticulated, pointing north:

"You must drive on, please."

Out by the standing stones, a figure was taking in the view out over the Loch of Harray, his hands behind his back. A pair of clumsy ducks splashed down on the water.

"I would like to speak to Mr Komolovsky."

"That is not possible."

"I am Inspector Roland Clett from Kirkwall Police station."

The woman examined Clett's Volkswagen Polo, spotted with rust and a mismatched door from an old accident.

"Really?"

Clett offered his ID; she lifted her wrist to her mouth, speaking Russian into a hidden microphone. Beyond, the figure at the stones waved.

"Mr Komolovsky will speak with you."

"That's very nice of him."

As Clett parked the Polo, the bodyguard caught the attention of her colleague and wearily rolled her eyes. The other shrugged. Clett followed a single set of footprints on the new snow to the old stones, the familiar patterns of scoring on each one highlighted in white.

"Mr Komolovsky? My name is…"

"I know who you are. Inspector Clett. I saw you and your wife at the restaurant, at the Foveran. I think you left in a hurry."

"We ate somewhere else."

"No; I am sure it was my companion. It was the presence of Mister Rust that upset you. You and your wife were uncomfortable, I think."

"A little, yes."

"Your wife is a very attractive woman."

"Indeed, I'm sure she…"

"Do you know Mister Rust well?"

Clett puffed out and shook his head. The Russian scanned the gleaming horizon.

"I have heard that these islands, they are small. Everybody knows somebody."

"They are. They do. I was at school with Ronnie Rust."

"Ah. I would like it very much if you could tell me more about him, please."

"What is your interest in him?"

"It is an old story. He has political ambitions, I have money."

"I would have thought you had bigger fish to fry."

"Forgive me, I do not understand."

"You know, your own concerns are more, how shall I say, more global."

"I like it here. These are good people. Mister Rust has a desire to do good in Orkney."

Clett chuckled.

"You really believe that Ronnie Rust wants to do good?"

"Yes, I do. Do you question my judgement?"

"There are many people on these islands who hold Ronnie Rust in high regard."

"But I think perhaps you can tell a different story about Mister Rust."

"I'm sorry Mr Komolovsky, I cannot say more until I know why you are interested in Ronnie Rust."

"That is fair. He needs a sponsor to finance his local political ambitions. I need more information about him before I make a commitment. All I hear is good; this man has redeemed himself; he has extricated himself from a criminal life and wishes the best for his community. A story that is close to my heart. How shall I say it? It is my own story."

Clett kicked lightly at the snow banked against one of the standing stones.

"Forget what you have heard, Mr Komolovsky; what is your feeling of the man?"

"You prefer the Socratic method, Inspector. I like that. Let me see. Mister Rust is, how shall I put it? He is unsubtle. But I have done business with many unsubtle men in my life."

"So why not just do your business, just like you have done with these other men?"

"You have me, Inspector. You must understand, I am interested now in other things. It is, you see, much more to me than the mere issue of profit. I have bought a fine little football club, Falkirk Albion. You know this, I think. I have followed them for some years now, and I wish to make a future for these boys, the same as I want to make a future for the people of Orkney. I like these islands; I would like to facilitate the business of good here. Maybe I build a home here."

"Really? They say that there are other reasons for investing in such projects."

"Ah, what you call 'money laundering'. What can I say, Inspector? I invest in things that interest me; I obey the law. When my advisors tell me there is a way to make more money, I listen to them. I am that kind of animal."

"You regard Ronnie Rust as a foot in the door?"

"Again, I am sorry, Inspector, I do not understand."

"No Mr Komolovsky, it is I who should apologise. I mean to say that I suspect that you see Ronnie Rust as an agent for your project to do good here."

"Exactly so, Inspector. You have, how do you say, hit the screw on the head."

"And you want an opinion about his character from someone who has known him for many years."

"Inspector, we understand each other."

"Ok. Let me ask you a question. What do you think is Ronnie Rust's motivation?"

"As I say, he wants to do good for the people around him."

"Really?"

"Absolutely. As I say to you, Inspector, I have met men like him. Their desire is redemption; their way of achieving it is to benefit others."

Clett's eyes opened wide.

"I feel you are about to introduce a caveat here."

"Indeed, I am. Inspector. I can be honest with you? Yes?"

The two men looked towards the security staff at the perimeter of the Stones of Stenness site. Komolovsky waved them away, and they disappeared into their cars, leaving the Russian and Clett alone, surrounded by snow and the limestone columns that had stood for five thousand years, that had seen many such debates about the intentions of men.

"When these men want to do good, they make promises. They are assiduous – is that the correct word, Inspector?"

"It is a good word Mr Komolovsky."

"Yes, Inspector. These men are assiduous in the pursuit of their cause. They come from a world, such a world of unspeakable violence, that their souls demand compensations. They could not but strive to pay for the things they did in their past. So, they make their promises and they meet their exact deadlines and targets. You should know that how they keep their promises is the key. They pursue solutions using their old skills. You have a saying, I think, 'old habits are hard to kill'."

"'Die hard', the phrase is 'old habits die hard'."

"As you say. These men could not but resort to a total management of their situations. Nothing can get in their way. They will do anything to keep their promises."

"You think Ronnie Rust is one of these men."

"Well, you tell me, Inspector? You have known him longer than I."

"This is an interesting perspective."

"I have made myself an expert on such men. I have had to know them; you understand me? Yes?"

Komolovsky brushed away some snow, fingering the yellow lichen on the surface of the limestone pinnacle that towered above them.

"There is more, Inspector. Would you like me to continue?"

"Please."

"I know what I have done in my own past Inspector, things about which I am not happy. But I am lucky man, I am very lucky man. I have been allowed opportunities to remedy my sins."

He stroked the lichen through the frost, soft and at the same time, spiky.

"I use my influence to detach myself from people in my past, perhaps by means I am not proud of. As such I have positioned myself in a place where I can choose where my energies are directed."

"People like Ronnie Rust?"

"Like Mister Rust, yes, they will use all their skills to achieve their outcomes, the ends of this good they seek. I know. I have also done it; I see that same potential in Mister Rust."

Clett put his hands in his pockets and scanned the stones and beyond, north to the Ring of Brodgar, also dusted white. Overhead, a skein of geese honked through the sky.

"Mr Komolovsky let me tell you a thing or two about Ronnie Rust. He began with minor acts of mere badness: shooting livestock, bullying at school and so on. Then ran a tobacco smuggling operation between Norway and Orkney. He once keelhauled two young boys because he thought they were stealing from him; these lads nearly died. I am currently investigating his role in the murder of a young man at an archaeological dig site on Westray in April, and he was charged with a particularly nasty assault on a young woman at his nightclub. This man represents all that evil is, but he uses his skills to demonstrate to the people of these islands that he is an honest man who can work for them. It appears that I am the only person who can perceive his real nature."

"I see your dilemma, Inspector. You must do what you must, but I tell you as an honest man that I have seen myself how such a man can do good things."

"And I tell you that this man will never change. All he offers is a facade of humanity. I agree that he may have a distorted motivation, to do something that is a facsimile of good, but as long as that motivation is driven by an uncompromising rationale, driven by a non-negotiable force that relies on a propensity for evil, this community can never be truly safe from such a person."

Komolovsky slapped Clett on the shoulder and gestured with his other hand to the odd shaped ship out in Kirkwall Bay.

"Do you like my cruiser, Inspector? It is 'Vorona'."

Clett considered the boat, its black bulk dominating the grey-white landscaped vista to the east. Its profile was not that of a boat, but, from this angle, like a huge dark bird.

"It doesn't look like a boat."

"I had it designed by Philipp Starke in Paris."

"So you say."

"You are a hard man to impress, Inspector."

Clett ran his finger down a groove in one of the huge columns in the nearest standing stone, pressing his palm against the cold limestone. Komolovsky caught his glance.

"You would say it is necessary for a person to engage with others, where that person reaches conclusions dependent on, how shall I say... dependent on mutual rational agreement. I do not believe such a thing. I believe that the true nature of compromise is that people must accept the rule of a strong individual who is motivated to do good; and sometimes that individual may have to take decisions that are... unpalatable."

"Mr Komolovsky, yours is the Russian way. This is Orkney."

"Inspector, the Russian people have lived with such contrasts in outlook for hundreds of years. It is rooted deep in the human condition; it is embedded in the Russian soul. I would say that your culture in the West has suffered because you deny this dichotomy that reflects our true nature. I would also observe that you seem not to recognise the redemption that can exist in others."

As clouds raced overhead, the light dimmed. They walked back towards the cars.

"Mr Komolovsky, I am a policeman. If I recognise the potential for criminal behaviour, I must address it."

"Ah, Inspector, I do not think that you give yourself credit for your philosophical sensitivity."

"Ha! If my wife could hear you, she would laugh."

"Indeed. I would like to meet your wife, Inspector."

Clett waved to the pair of blacked out SUVs as they drove south and east, back to Hatston in the direction of Komolovsky's black 'Vorona'. A new fall of thick snow was coming down, making the world a blur of white. Clett shivered and opened the door of the still warm Polo, turning the key. He lifted a thin folder on the passenger seat and took a photocopy of one of Archibald Clett's letters, scribbling notes as he read.

> *To David Hume Esq.*
> *1 St David Street*
> *Edinburgh*
> *7th June 1742*
> *My Dear Friend,*
>
> *My fecund sheep have lambed, and I have twenty-one new youngsters. Which they should keep me in profit this year. It is a joy to see them perform their wee leaps as they perambulate my parks.*
>
> *Last night, I slept poorly and rose lonely without my Mary to keep me warm. I lit a fire and turned to your last letter about sin – and forgiveness of one's own sins. I made a note which I copy here:*
>
> *There is in one's own reaction to our misdeeds, a spectrum of response. On one side of that spectrum, there is a keenness for a fight, a need to exert force, a recognition that one's position is justified, a need to have power over the fates. And at the other side there is also the silent, turning in upon one's self*

where there is such guilt for our action that it can indeed lead to death.

These responses offer a compass of shame that is manifested in all our responses to sin. I would observe that the shame we experience varies, and that we each have our own propensity to each of these reactions in a different manner. One person may be shocked into inaction by a minor sin, and another will seem to be unaffected. This compass of shame forms a moral element in that field of ideas about our sin and our governance of it. Once again, we have identified something of the sentiment of morality that exists within us all.

Yrs, louing Friend, Arch. Clett of Canmore

Outside the car, the snow cleared. Clett watched a huge cylinder of grey snow move over the water on Kirkwall bay, obscuring Komolovsky's 'Vorona'.

$$
\begin{array}{c}
\text{O} \\
\| \\
\text{HO} - \text{S} - \text{OH} \\
\| \\
\text{O}
\end{array}
$$

vitriol

Mergret Isbister's Studio, Lopness
Monday 30th November 1942

Charlotte shared a cigarette with Mergret Isbister, their mouths agape at what was in front of them. A barrage balloon had come adrift from its moorings in Scapa Flow and blown north, all the way to Sanday. Charlotte had observed its slow progress on her screen during her shift, and now, it was overhead. There was a worry that it would collide with the aerial masts at Whale Head. Outside, in the clear sunshine, people looked up at the huge shapeless mass of hydrogen, enclosed in silk and bamboo, tumbling, rolling through the sky, trailing its quarter-inch steel hawser along the ground. Charlotte thought about her night with Jim. Hoy seemed a hundred years ago. Would the islands sink just a little without the support of a single blimp?

"Is she not beautiful?" said Mergret.

"I expect they'll send a couple of Hurricanes to shoot it down."

"Surely they won't waste the ammo?"

Above them, the leviathan rolled and yawed, upending itself, turning over, rotating around the point where it was attached to the guy. A flock of terns rose in its path and split, the balloon changing its shape as the hydrogen moved inside its envelope. As they watched, there was a sound of aircraft engines from the south.

"Told you so. They'll use it for a spot of target practice, I reckon."

Charlotte and Mergret watched as two Hurricanes approached, flying around the blimp, gambolling, banking this way and that, circling, swooping over and under their target. They split and flew a distance before returning to attack, their guns rattling the sky. They strafed the balloon, and it disintegrated above Scuthvie Bay. Charlotte and Mergret felt the heat of the invisible explosion of gas, strips of silk floating in every direction.

"I thought there would be flames."

"You can't see Hydrogen when it burns."

A large piece of silk floated down and became snagged on one of the limestone fenceposts Orcadians used instead of wood. Mergret carefully detached the material from the jagged rock.

"That'll do to keep the hay dry. Here."

She gave the sheet of silk to Charlotte who felt the soft texture between her fingers. A motorcycle approached.

"Miss? Charlotte Hall?"

"Hello Freddy. Did you see the blimp? Wasn't it beautiful?"

Freddy coughed and looked to the ground.

"Yes, miss. Miss, I've got a telegram."

The blood drained from Charlotte's face and she stumbled. Mergret took her arm.

"Thank you, Freddy. I'll take it."

"I'm sorry miss."

Charlotte's head was spinning. A telegram? Who was it? Had they bombed Shere?

Charlotte took the thin envelope, feeling for the flap. She tore at the paper.

> **FROM ADMIRALTY DEEPLY**
> **REGRET DEATH OF LIEUTENANT**
> **JAMES THOMAS MANNERS STOP**
> **KILLED ON ACTIVE SERVICE**
> **LETTER TO FOLLOW STOP**

"What does it mean?"

Mergret read the telegram.

"Is he your sweetheart?"

"Yes, but he can't be dead. There must be a mistake. We were together. We were in Lyness."

The world swam in Charlotte's vision. From where they sat, they saw the whole of Whale Head, its towers, its little trucks and vehicles on duckboards, in the mud, going about their business, and out past Lopness, the old wreck of a First World War German Cruiser. To the south, the dark presence of Start Point Lighthouse, now hidden, camouflaged to make it invisible. How topsy-turvy the war made this world; who would disguise a lighthouse? Instead of warning people, instead of keeping them safe, it let death happen.

"He just can't be dead."

Mergret turned the telegram over.

"These bloody, bloody things. They never give you enough information."

Charlotte shivered, chilled by the loss of heat from a large cloud that covered the sun. She held the silk from the barrage balloon in one hand, and the telegram envelope in the other, unaware of any weight. Mergret touched Charlotte's shoulder, guiding her back towards the farm, and the studio.

"This way, dear. Let's get you a cup of tea. There's fresh milk."

To the south, the horizon seemed lower in the sky.

Papa Rousay
Sunday 19th December 2010

Jerzy Przybylski stepped off the open boat and looked back over the, two hundred metres over the narrow strip of water. The current was picking up. He had been taken across the channel by Brother Francisco, an American monk, wearing sea boots and a yellow waterproof jacket that just covered his cassock. Jerzy attempted conversation.

"When the tide is strong it must be difficult to get here, Brother."

"Not really. Call me Cyd."

Cyd tied up the boat. The sun came out from a gap in the clouds. To the side of the jetty was a huge mound of large scallop shells covered in snow, reflecting the intense light. Cyd covered his eyes.

"Mass is about to start."

Jerzy followed the American to the whitewashed chapel, a modern functional structure. Inside, he immediately engaged with the Latin ritual, standing, kneeling and muttering the familiar chants. After the service, he stood beside Cyd looking back across the channel. Jerzy pointed.

"There's a seal."

Cyd grunted, "Buddy, when you live here these critters are an everyday sight."

"Oh."

They walked down to the beach in silence. Across the water was the little harbour, and along the road, the village of Whitehall. A fishing boat was chugging out towards the sea, trailing smoke and wake. The skipper waved at the two men.

"You said in your email you want to talk to us about redemption. You could have communicated on the web, skyped even, but you've come all the way from Krakow?"

"Yes. I wanted to see this place for myself."

Over the water, a pair of gulls squawked.

"You and your website have created waves in this community. We have just had a very traumatic split over theological matters. You're lucky that people here will give you the time of day. We've had these discussions online; they are pointless, we're going round in circles."

"I appreciate it, but I wanted to speak to you directly."

"Ok you're here now, shoot."

"Your model of redemption is by the sole use of prayer."

"You know our position on this. We do not accept that prayer can actually be used for anything. It has no function as such. All it does is open conduits for God's love."

"Yes, but you see no other way of redeeming a soul than by prayer?"

Cyd wearily kicked stones from the beach.

"That would be an abbreviated statement of our beliefs, yes."

"And no other means? For instance, through the personal sacrifice of another's soul."

"For example?"

"Well, if someone were to abrogate their right to enter the kingdom of Heaven for another person, say."

"Why would anyone do that?"

"I don't know, I suppose as an ultimate act of giving to another person."

"Just how would you do it?"

"Through a small ritual event."

"And you call yourself a priest?"

"Not any more, not in the formal sense."

"You, that is, that person, would have the effrontery to assume God's role, to decide who was to benefit from his divine gift? Only Jesus can make such a sacrifice. Mere mortals can have no such role. At the very best, certain of us have the privilege of being allowed to be a channel for God's will. When we offer absolution at confession or at the last rites, we do so through God. We are not acting as free agents but through the mechanism of God's will. Any such interference in this is sinful."

"But what if I wish to make such a sacrifice? What if I want to take on the sins of others to give that ultimate gift?"

"You mean like dying for the sins of others? You must know what you are saying. It's blasphemy. You cannot take it upon yourself to choose who may or may not enter the kingdom of heaven."

"I know, but I have a need to help others."

Jerzy paused, looking out to the lapping tide. A dog splashed in the surf and tried to bite the water.

* * *

"Good morning Inspector; any more evidence on your Moriarty?"

"Who?"

"You know, your arch-enemy, Mister Rust."

The sound of sniggering came from the other side of the office.

"I, eh…"

"It's ok sir, it's just banter," said Nancie Keldie.

"Aye."

Clett went to his desk and closed his eyes. He ran his hands over its surface, feeling the old carvings and graffiti under his fingertips; the rings and creatures and strange writing created by people before him, but utterly familiar; this unreadable script that once made sense to someone. And today, he was being ridiculed. What had he done to deserve this? These people, once so close, now betraying him, talking behind his back, telling jokes? Clett breathed slowly, focussing on his visualisations, telling himself he was imagining it all. At least that was what he knew he had to believe. Only in this denial of his feelings about these scenarios was he going to remain sane. He knew if he gave in to these thoughts of persecution and ridicule that it would fuel the torment that had brought him down before. He forced himself to repeat in his head: "Is it really the case that these people conspire and plot behind your back when they have worries of their own?"

He stared out the window to the spire of St Magnus Cathedral. In the old days, truth was in books and supplied by priests. But now, you could buy into some half-baked solution from the bookshelf, or you could spend your life working it out for yourself. This was the way Clett was. He had worked out his own moral narrative, tested in the ambiguous world of police work. He had concluded that there was no good or evil and that people reacted to circumstance; that rules and the law were guidelines, a scaffolding for the institutions that society relied upon. All these rules amounted to a story; the stories that people collectively believed but had little to do with the actual motivations behind the actions of men and women. The actions of people were bounded by circumstance, not laws. So when Clett had to accept the narrative of others – in this case for the sake of his sanity – this was in opposition to the method he had developed over the years. He was torn between relying on his own judgement, and the authority of a psychologist who told him that the loss of his sanity would be the price he would pay for the continued exercise of his intuition. If he continued to act on his delusions, he could not continue working, and his long-term mental health would be seriously at risk.

Here was Clett's dilemma; either approach the job in a robotic fashion, blindly following procedure, or allow himself to solve problems intuitively. The first approach would ensure his mental stability but diminish his effectiveness as a policeman; the second might well lead to a breakdown.

* * *

Clett opened the door of the Orkney Room, nodding to the man at the archive reception.

"Afternoon, Arthur."

"Afternoon Roland. Would you like to look at the Archibald Clett archive?"

"Yes Arthur; the usual. Thanks."

"Take a seat."

Clett took a seat, surrounded by old Orkney books. The atmosphere calmed him; breathing slowly, he looked out the window to the spire of Saint Magnus Cathedral.

Arthur returned, pushing a trolley containing a box file marked 'Arch. Clett — Canmore, (1721—1799). Inside were three buff folders marked 'Translations and Correspondence 1742 to 1799', one marked 'Grand Tour 1741/2', and another, 'Misc.'

Clett took the miscellaneous file and opened it. It had the

uncatalogued items from the Archibald Clett collection. At the top of the pile of sheets of faded paper was Archibald Clett's translation of an epic poem from 1642 by the French poet Rolande de Ville d'Fin, entitled 'Le Mythe du Cordelière'. Clett put it aside and found the letter he was looking for. He scanned the criss-cross writing that covered both sides of the small piece of paper. To anyone looking at it for the first time, the writing was indecipherable, just a jumble of scribbles, but Clett had taught himself how to interpret it. Archibald Clett had used this method as a record of his correspondence, copying all his letters in abbreviated forms, writing first in one direction, then diagonally over the previous writing. This was, however, not a letter, but a page torn from a notebook.

> *I have today received a visitor to my little home at Canmore whom I have found to be the most disturbing of companions. He presented at the funeral which I attended of my old neighbour, Old John Sinclair of Gyre – Requiescat &c. The visitor was a slight man with pale skin and a thin wiry beard. He came to Old John's widow, Jessie, and whispered in her ear. She looked at the man, nodded, and invited him to the home privately and all present made way for him. He was a chameleon-like man with a hushed southern accent, almost incomprehensible. I felt sure that he was a sin-eater that I had heard visited at funerals and saved people from purgatory. Jessie spoke Norn[4] to him, and he understood. All around were still, and not one moved, even when the light rain started up. After a while, he came out of Old John's house and we all moved out of his way, like droplets of water falling from a bird's feather. Not one looked him in the eye and he walked away.*
>
> *After the wake, I walked home and as I approached Canmore, I saw him again and I invited him for food which he accepted. We sat at my table and I asked him many questions, but he made little response. He said his name was Judas. I asked him:*

---

[4] Norn was the ancient language spoken in Orkney. It died out in the eighteenth century.

"They say you are giving away your soul by consuming the sins of others."
He just ate his bread and beer in silence.
"Why do you do this thing?"
At no time did he regard me. I gave him some pennies and he said one thing that I nearly could not apprehend but I wrote it after:
"There is a wind of fate that blows through time, and people have no control over it. We are all destined to be sinners, but it is how we redeem ourselves is what makes us able to share this space on this little earth for this little time. In our shame is our redemption."
Then he left my home. I was happy to see him go and I do not wish to see him again.

The note was undated. Possibly around 20th December 1746. Clett wrote on his copy: 'see letter to Murdo Mackenzie of that date'.

* * *

Christine Clett lifted an envelope that had been posted through the front door. It was addressed to her in scrawly block capitals and had no stamp.

DECEMBER 12 2010
DEAR MRS CLETT I HOPE YOU REMEMBER ME YOU TAUGHT ME IN PRIMARY 7. CEDRIC SINCLAIR WAS MY FRIEND THE OTHER CHILDREN CALLED HIM PIGGY AND WE STAYED FRIENDS EVER SINCED. I ALWAYS REMEMBERED YOU AND YOU ALWAYS LISTENED TO US AND I SEEN YOU AROUND KIRKWALL A FEW TIMES AND YOU ALWAYS SAID HELLO SO I THINK YOU WILL REMEMBER ME I AM WRITING TO YOU BECAUSE I AM IN A LOT OF TROUBLE ME AND CEDRIC WERE WORKING FOR MISTER RUST ON ONE OF HIS FISHING BOATS LAST YEAR AND HE ASKED US TO CARRY SOME PACKAGES FOR HIM. WE DID WHAT HE SAID AND HE GAVE US SOME MONEY AND

THEN WE LOST THE PACKAGE OVER THE SIDE AND MISTER RUST THOUGHT WE STOLE IT. HE TOOK US OUT TO SEA AND TIED ROPES TO OUR HANDS AND FEET AND USED THEM TO PULL US BOTH UNDER THE WATER THE TWO OF US THOUGHT WE WERE GOING TO DIE. MISTER RUST IS A VERY BAD MAN AND I THINK THAT NO ONE ON ORKNEY KNOWS THIS CEDRIC AND ME DONT TALK ANYMORE WE ARE FRIGHTENED MISTER RUST WILL HURT US AGAIN CEDRIC HAS GONE TO LIVE SOMEWHERE ELSE I LIVE IN BURRAY NOW I SAW MISTER RUST OPENING THE NEW SPORTS CENTRE THERE AND I THINK HE SAW ME I AM SO SCARED MRS CLETT YOU WERE ALWAYS SO KIND TO US AND I DONT KNOW WHO ELSE TO SAY THESE THINGS TO PLEASE LOOK AFTER THIS LETTER AND IF ANYTHING HAPPENS TO ME PLEASE GIVE IT TO THE POLICE I AM VERY FRIGHTENED THANK YOU FOR EVERYTHING YOURS TRULY JOHN FLEAR

* * *

Ronnie Rust opened the cupboard and chose polish and brushes. Five pairs of shoes were laid out on the kitchen floor. Three were his own, two belonging to Auntie Brenda.

He took the oxblood polish, and the Dymo-labelled 'ON' brush, and he lifted a shoe, a left brogue, a beautiful shade of burgundy. He applied the thick waxy polish, covering the whole shoe in a thin film of the dense deep-red cream: first the brogue itself, on the toe, over the apron, round the vamp to the instep, and working around the heel, before repeating the process on the right shoe. He put away the oxblood, and opened the tin of black polish, remembering the games of peever, where he played a polish tin along the ground, like a stone. It all depended on the tin. The older it was, the better, and you could reduce the friction on the tin by rubbing it on a stone surface. Rust smiled at the memory. He lifted a black loafer, first the left shoe, gently and meticulously rubbing until the finish was dulled with the unbuffed polish. Then, repeating the ritual with the right shoe, placing them next to the brogues. Next was a pair of Chelsea boots with a mid-tan. Returning to the brogues, the polish now embedded in the grain of the leather, he took a brush labelled 'OFF' and buffed the left brogue. Starting at the toe, and in a practised oscillation of his wrist, he brushed the apron and the sides. He spat on the apron and carried on brushing until the shoe shone. Shifting the shoe on his left hand, turning it so the brushing now covered the instep, and the outer edge, and in a continuous motion around to the heel, he repeated the process with a lighter stroke, admiring it, placing it beside its partner. Carrying out the same ritual, he continued, working on the pair of black loafers, then on his Chelsea boots. He considered his footwear, pleasant and pristine, like new, and bent to lift one of Brenda's scuffed shoes, a ladies' leather moccasin. He placed his hand inside the shoe to apply the polish, feeling the cold damp leather, the worn heel, the fragments of leather, rubbed away by years of contact with Brenda's foot. Rust held the shoe at a distance, trying not to breathe in the familiar odour. He turned his head away and applied the polish. That odour. Rust's father had taught him how to polish shoes. Every Friday, Ronnie would polish everyone's shoes, leaving his father's until last, the shoes that his father would wear that night; the shoes that he would later take off when he returned smelling of sweet beer. With the removal of his shoes, came the inevitable explosion of violence, his father screaming and spitting at the young boy, taking Ronnie by the ear, jamming his face against the warm, reeking leather…

Rust finished applying polish to Auntie Brenda's moccasins and picked up an old brown knee-high boot with platform heels. He placed his arm inside the right boot, the cold clammy damp interior reeking of that essence of Auntie Brenda, that flavour of her that Rust could never forget. He gagged, carrying on, his left arm inside the old worn, flabby leather. But the more he held it, the more he worked the leather, the heat from his arm warmed the inside of the boot, and the old reek came alive. Rust caressed her boot and the smell of old sweat became less bitter; he stroked the creases in the hide, gently massaging the polish into the leather. He placed the boot on the floor, and lifted its partner, again trying not to breathe in the cold stale stink; yet, as the boot warmed on his arm, he relaxed and fell into a stupor of sordid memory:

'Are you Daddy's boy? You little cunt.'

The blend of warm terror, the adventure of the next thing that Daddy was going to do, was everything. It was the fear, it was the joy, it was the love, it was the dread that inhabited the life of young Ronnie Rust. And here it was, right now, still tender, redolent in his kitchen, in the dizzy vapour of warm, fetid leather.

CHAPTER ELEVEN

testosterone

Mergret Isbister's Studio, Lopness
Saturday 5th December 1942

Charlotte's grief was played out in a continuous sequence of tea and 'Craven A' cigarettes. She refused leave and spent her waking moments at her screen, trying to distinguish enemy aircraft in the clutter. She read up on training notes on target detection and assessment. When she wasn't working, she slept. At least, she stayed in her bunk, away from people. This was how she dealt with her loss. She and Jim had only seen each other a handful of times, but they both knew they belonged together. All that stuff about a wartime fling; but that was not for them. They were to be with each other forever. They had talked of normal expectations of a shared future. She had practiced writing her new name – Charlotte Manners — it had a nice ring to it. They had even laughed about having children. Her heart was torn asunder.

Mergret gave her food not on the ration cards: bacon, butter, cheese, eggs, fresh milk. The one compensation for forces personnel posted to Orkney was the generosity of the local people who had access to the finest produce. This and the lilt of Mergret's Orkney voice, talking about art and technique, offered a peace that allowed her to have a place separate from her grief and her working existence. Mergret worked around Charlotte as she sat quietly, listening, dozing before returning for her shift.

The artist rummaged in a drawer for a postcard or in a book for an image:

"This is the kind of thing I am trying to capture, see this tone, here..."

Charlotte nodded and returned to looking out to the next phase of the weather.

One afternoon Mergret was sizing a canvas, painting white on white.

"Have you had any more contact with that young Private? Is he still pestering you?"

"Private Long? No. Not since he sent me that horrible poem. I used to think he was nice, but I don't know what to say to him now. I've never encouraged him, you know. I don't know what to do. Whale Head isn't that big, and I can't avoid him forever."

"You can come here any time, my dear." Mergret patted Charlotte's hand.

"I know. Where else could I get such lovely rations? A lot of us complain about Orkney; did you read that piece in *The Orkney Blast* about 'Bloody Orkney'? it's just so... so ungrateful, but now you know, since I've lost Jim, I just can't..."

Charlotte sniffed and wiped away a tear.

"Now he's gone, I don't want to be anywhere else."

Mergret touched Charlotte's shoulder for a moment.

"Can you see this painting? I'm trying to get these two images to live in the same space, see, the balance..."

Charlotte sat in Mergret's studio observing the older woman move around; bustling, trying a brush, or mixing colours, or sitting still in front of a part-formed image breathing in the air of tobacco smoke and turpentine. Charlotte dozed off and dreamt about the aurora borealis, standing in the clear night air, looking up at the infinite forms of light, changing in their silent violence, splitting the night sky into division, and she heard Jim's voice, incoherent, words indistinct, just his cadence, followed by his distant laughter.

Finstown
Monday 20th December 2010

Christine put down the iron, went upstairs to her bedside table and took John Flear's letter. She scanned it, folded it and put it in her pocket, lifted the car keys and went out. Clett watched the car rolling out of the drive. She took the fifteen-minute drive out of Finstown towards Kirkwall, with the bay of Firth on her left, fringed with the snow that now covered all of the Mainland. Paying no heed to the changing sky, she had taken this road hundreds of times before, and knew each turn and rise, but today the fresh fall of snow obscured all the landmarks. It was as if she was driving in a new landscape, with no defining features. She was unaware of the passage of time, when she found herself passing the Peedie Sea. Slowly, she drove along Harbour Street, meticulously indicating at each turn, and roundabout, past the marina and the tourist office, and out to the Olfsquoy estate. She turned into the quiet streets and stopped outside a house and turned off the engine. There was silence, the snow having taken all the sound from the air.

The house stood out from all the other houses in the estate. It was painted bright blue and had two plaster horse heads at the gateposts. In the large drive were parked two identical silver BMWs, with the registration RUS 5 and RUS 6.

Christine closed her car door and walked to the house and pressed the doorbell. A tall well-built man in an open zipped sweatshirt and a gold medallion opened the door.

"Mrs Inspector Clett. What a pleasant surprise."

Rust gestured to Christine.

"Why don't you come in?"

"I just wanted to have a word."

"Of course. I've seen your car here a few times. Have you been keeping an eye on me for that husband of yours?"

Rust smiled a broad grin.

They went into the lounge. A large television was showing a football match. Christine sat and raised her voice to be heard over the commentary.

"My husband and you go back a long time."

"Indeed we do. Man and boy. We lived on Papay until those kind social workers took me away."

"I want you to leave him alone."

"Why, I don't know what you mean Christine."

"Mrs Clett to you."

Rust smiled again.

"Anything you say, Mrs Clett."

"I want you to stay away from my husband."

Ronnie Rust reached across and patted Christine's knee. She flinched and swiped his hand away. Rust looked directly into her face.

"Look, Mrs Clett, I bear your husband no ill-will. Whatever he thinks of me, I have done him no harm whatsoever. I have actually helped his career. You didn't know that, did you? You see, I love this community, and I love these islands, and all I want is to serve these people."

Rust stood and looked out of his window out to the sea. Two island ferries passed each other on their north-south trajectories.

"Did you know I was running in the local elections?"

He handed Christine a pamphlet showing Rust shaking hands with another man.

"My husband has enough problems, and I need you to stay away from him."

"My dear Christine..."

"Mrs Clett."

"Mrs Clett, please... why would I wish your husband any harm?"

"I know what you are."

"Do you indeed?"

"I do. I know about John Flear. You knew him as Kermit, and his friend, Piggy."

"Silly boys with big imaginations."

"You nearly killed them. They are so traumatised that they may never hold down a job again."

Christine took the letter from her handbag.

"I have a letter from John Flear. He was a pupil of mine. He describes how you nearly killed those two boys out at sea. I will make a statement to the police, and I will write to the papers. How will that affect your political ambitions?"

Christine clutched the letter and his pamphlet in her fist. Out in Kirkwall Bay, the two ferries were now veering away from each other.

"Let's go for a walk, shall we."

He bent and took Christine's elbow, which she shook away from him.

"I just want you away from us."

He placed his hand firmly on her shoulder.

"Come outside. I want to show you something."

Ronnie Rust opened the front door and stood aside.

"After you, Mrs Clett."

They went out of the drive and along the street, silently walking along the slushy pavement. Christine put Rust's pamphlet in her pocket. In the other direction came an elderly lady with a shopping basket on wheels; she smiled.

"Good morning, Mister Rust."

"Good morning, Mrs Guthrie. How is your grandson? How did he get on at his exams?"

"Oh, Mister Rust, he did so well. He has a conditional to study medicine at Aberdeen. And all down to your help."

"Oh, anyone would have done it Mrs Guthrie."

"You are a saint Mister Rust. God bless you."

Rust patted the woman on the shoulder.

"Anybody would have done the same. You get away to the shops now."

Christine watched as the woman shuffled down the street.

"Do you see how it is, Mrs Clett? These people love me, and I want to give them something back."

"You mean like drugs and violence? Ronnie Rust, you are a thug and a gangster, and it is my husband's wish to protect the people of Orkney from you. So, you see, if you do not leave him alone, I will send John Flear's letter to the police."

Rust smiled down at Christine.

"Let's go down here to the beach."

They turned down a narrow lane towards the sea. There were no footprints in the snow that gently banked up at the edge towards the walls on either side. A cat approached from the other direction, leaving gentle depressions. Rust bent down to stroke it. Christine tried to keep her distance in the tiny lane.

"There you go puss, puss, puss. Beautiful, lovely cat you are."

Rust chucked the cat behind its ear, and it purred.

"You see Mrs Clett, your idea of me is wrong. Whatever you think I have done; this is the person I am."

"I have a letter that proves otherwise, and I intend to send it to the police."

"I see."

Rust smiled and lifted the cat by the neck. Instantly, it started spitting and hissing, clawing at the air. Rust held it at arm's length, close to Christine's face. She tried to move, but Rust's large frame blocked her way in the narrow-walled lane. Inches from her was the terrified spitting grasping creature, and behind, Rust's smiling face. He gripped the cat's throat tightly and squeezed. Its eyes bulged, and it yowled and squirmed and danced, trying to find purchase in the free air between Rust and Christine, who was frozen in horror at the sight of what he was doing to this poor creature.

"Stop. Don't..."

Rust put his other hand to his lips.

"Shhh."

He smiled and relaxed. Here he controlled all. He saw how the cat screwed itself below his grip, and he saw the fear in Christine's eyes. Rust grinned to himself; it was that moment: the cat looked at him and they both knew that he was not going to stop. He squeezed more, and the cat stopped struggling, and looked at him, knowing this was the end. Christine was crying as the creature made two more surges of effort to survive in Rust's grip.

"Stop, please stop."

The cat became limp in Rust's grip. In the narrow space of the lane, he stood close and stroked Christine's cheek with the warm coat of the dead animal. Christine shivered at its touch. She smelled Rust's aftershave and felt his breath on her face.

"Please, no," she whimpered.

"Now you see, Mrs Clett, how the Lord giveth, and the Lord taketh away. It is as easy and as simple as that."

Once more, he held the cat's body against Christine's cheek, then threw the body over a garden wall and walked away.

Christine remained, sobbing and shivering. She crouched down and put her face in her hand, looking up to see if Rust would return. What had happened? Was it somehow a dream? What had she just witnessed? It was simply not believable. She stood and looked up and down the silent lane. Out at sea, the ferry was heading in towards Kirkwall. Around her the simple depressions of footprints and scuffs in the snow the only evidence that this nightmare had been real.

* * *

"Good morning, Jerzy. We met at Lopness, on Sanday. I'm Inspector Roland Clett."

"I remember, Inspector. It is good to meet you once more."

Jerzy Przybylski had wide staring eyes and messy hair and an old waterproof jacket and jeans. It was difficult to tell his age, perhaps early thirties. Clett looked up from his file.

"Am I pronouncing your name correctly?"

"No Inspector. It is Shi-bil-ski."

"Shi-bil-ski."

"Correct, Inspector. Do not say the P in my name. You must call me Jerzy." Jerzy smiled to himself.

"Ok, Jerzy. When did you arrive on Orkney?"

"A week ago."

"I see. Do you mind me asking why you were on Sanday?"

"I am on holiday, Inspector. I like place where no people."

"Ok, and you just came by the body?"

"Sorry, can you repeat please?"

"You found the body by accident?"

"Of course."

"The bowl on his chest – the grey substance has been identified as salt."

Jerzy nodded.

"We are concerned that the body was interfered with. I think you might have placed that bowl on the body. Did you place that bowl on the body?"

"I not do this thing."

"If you are found to be lying, you may well be charged with perverting the course of justice."

Jerzy remained impassive. Clett looked at the sheets of paper in front of him.

"You are from Poland?"

"I am from Krakow. I was brought up at the foot of the Tatras. There are excellent mushrooms where I am from. I study Mathematics at Jagelonian University."

Jerzy paused, and then carried on slowly, deliberating on each word, appearing to examine Clett as he spoke.

"It is very spiritual thing, Mathematics."

"Do you think so?"

"Yes. I do think so. The first time I understand Euler's Relation, I feel presence of God in that small relation. It contains the five naturally occurring constants e, i, pi, 0 and 1. I weep when I see it."

"I see. Did you carry on with your mathematics?"

"There was always something not there. I wanted to do something for other people. The joy of mathematics was joy inside, but did not do any good for people, you know?"

"Yes. I understand."

"Other arts – music, poetry, painting – can all be shared with others, but mathematics had no moral place. I needed to do something for other people."

Jerzy had a sip of water from a plastic cup.

"As a boy I was taught to hold open doors for others. My father said that I must always do things for other people before I do things for myself. The needs of other people are always more important than my own needs. But then I learned to be priest. It made my parents very proud."

"But you didn't you stay in the priesthood? It would seem the ideal role for you."

"Ah, Inspector, there is my curse. I am not always as you see me today. Today, here, I know the rules. You ask me questions and I answer them. This series of transactions I understand. But out there…"

Jerzy waved his hand in the direction of the window.

"Out there the world is so much more complicated. Out there, people do not just ask questions, and if they do ask questions, they are not the questions that they think they are asking, and the answers you give them are not the answers to the questions they think they have asked. And I have no way of thinking about the unasked questions that are present when they speak."

Clett raised his eyebrows.

"Really; and what is that unasked question?"

"It is different for everyone. And I have constantly tried to give, what is that old word in English – 'succour'."

"I have to say that I can't see why you have a problem with your communications but…"

"Inspector, these rules we have today. It is a game. Today's rules are fixed, and we are playing by them, but outside that door there are many games going on at once and I cannot deal with that. People speak with their bodies and their eyes, and this I cannot understand; and if I cannot understand them, I cannot do what I seem fated to do. So, I am a contradiction. I must be so, but I am denied the opportunity to be so."

Clett sat back in his seat.

"Well Jerzy, I am sorry for your situation."

Jerzy sat forward in his chair and caught Clett's gaze.

"But you Inspector; I think that you are not content."

Clett stopped. "Interview terminated at 15.45 on 21st December 2010."

He fiddled with the cassettes, removed them and gave one to

Jerzy. "This is yours. If you wish to speak to a lawyer, he may wish to listen to it."

Jerzy reached over the table and touched Clett's elbow.

"You are troubled man, no?"

"Aren't we all, Jerzy?"

Jerzy stayed still, keeping his gaze on Clett.

"Are you loved?"

"Yes. I am. I am loved."

"But you do not love yourself?"

Clett fiddled with the other cassette, turning it over.

"No."

"But you are successful man, no?"

"I suppose so. It's complicated."

"It is always complicated."

"It's not professional for us to talk like this."

"But it might be useful."

Outside some crows cawed.

"I don't trust myself."

"Why so?"

"I have a particular perspective on a set of events, but no one else shares that perspective."

"Do these other people share your knowledge of these events you speak of?"

"No, but they have equally viable narratives of the situation that offer very different conclusions. There is a large number of these people."

Jerzy took the cassette tape of the interview and turned it over in his hand.

"Do you think you are losing your mind, Inspector Clett?"

"I think I am, but I cannot afford to accept that. Too many people rely on me."

"I see. And your narrative of these events, how confident are you that you are correct?"

Clett paused; a dog barked in the street outside.

"I am one hundred percent positive."

"Then, Inspector, I do not think you are losing your mind. In time, only one conclusion will come out of these events you speak of. Even when a conclusion to this becomes clear, you can still not truly know if what you think is true. Many people think that truth is absolute.

It is not. We live in a world of contradictory narratives. Most of us develop, what is the word... ah yes, we develop strategies to... to... to accommodate these... these contradictions. Sometimes we can avoid the individuals that hold the contradictory narrative. I assume you are not in a position to do this."

"No."

"I see. Well, you must evolve this narrative to ensure your own survival. If you have worked so hard to believe this, you must continue."

* * *

Clett opened his eyes. The clock showed quarter-past-three. He took a deep breath, staring at the light from the full moon on the ceiling, reflected off the snow through the open curtains. Clett rubbed his eyes and listened to the silence. No traffic noise, and only the sound of Christine's breathing. He thought of the day he had had, of how he had dealt with the teasing from his colleagues, of the repeated words going round and round in his head. His heart was racing; he was never going to get back to sleep. He tried his relaxation exercises but still came back to these imaginary arguments with people that meant him no harm. He started to doze a little, and dreamed he heard a noise downstairs; he got up and looked out of the window. There at the end of the garden, sitting on a flagstone fencepost was a barn owl, its body turned away from him, but with its head rotated about ninety degrees, looking straight at him. Just as their shared realisation became real, the owl fell forward, opening its wings, gliding along the ground as it slowly flapped and gained speed and height. It headed in the direction of the loch and away. Clett returned to bed and closed his eyes.

An hour later, Clett was still awake. He went to his desk and rifled through some of Archibald's letters, with their familiar overwriting, first left to right, then top to bottom, and then diagonally across the page. He took the last letter he had transcribed and re-read it. It concerned a plan to use ship's rigging as a signalling system. Ridiculous to a modern mind, but typical of the wide-ranging scope of Archibald's intellect, and his failures. He considered Archibald's error, and the feeling of humiliation he must have felt.

Clett considered his own situation. Rust's freedom, poor Geraldine's fragmenting life, and his own loss of control over events.

He looked out once more over the snow-covered garden. The

owl had returned and was peering at Clett. It blinked one eye and rotated its head to see over the garden. It resumed its gaze, stock still. Clett remained immobile, not wishing to change the moment. The two creatures regarded each other in their shared incoherence. How did the other see the world? What gave the other comfort? What was important? All these things so different for each of these creatures, separated by the glass window: each a reflection of the other. Inside, Clett's mess of a desk, with notes stuck on his computer screen, his attempt to resolve his troubles; and outside, the clean soft surface of snow, with this single predator.

Clett went over the circumstances surrounding the murder of Dominic Byrd at Noup Head. He had failed to understand something fundamental about that night of 21st April. What was it that DI Tony Nelson had said? Had he been right all along? Was de Vries involved in supplying drugs after all?

Outside, a car door closed. Clett went to the window where he saw Rust's car, across the road. He froze and watched, unbelieving as the silver BMW silently rolled away, putting its lights on just as it reached the main road. 'What on earth was Rust doing here?'

Clett quickly went out, started the Polo and slowly followed Rust's car west. He drove gingerly, at a distance, while considering the story that DI Tony Nelson had told about the death of Dominic Byrd, all those months ago. Despite Clett's dislike of the man, he now had to re-evaluate his story. He said that Dominic Byrd had been killed because of a drugs deal gone wrong. If that was so, Trevor de Vries was also involved – the dig team leader who had been a prime suspect and had subsequently committed suicide while in custody – and there was this new financial information linking him to Mexico. Clett was re-thinking this old story when Rust's car turned towards the Bay of Skaill. Clett followed north, and then west along the Lyking Road across the Bay of Stenness. He slowed as Rust took the single-track road towards Yesnaby where there were only the cliffs and the Atlantic Ocean. He turned his lights off, and followed the tyre tracks ahead, clear in the moon-lit snow. Then he came to the wide-open cliff top, covered in the ancient flagged stone floor. Clett stopped the car, keeping the engine running to stay warm. He relaxed and started to dream, unable to keep his eyes open. He looked at his watch, it was 4.33 am. In front of him was Rust's silver BMW, facing out to the north Atlantic, just by the old bunker, parked on the fifty feet of broken flagstones lit by the intermittent moon reflecting off piles of snow. Over the cliff was a 200-foot drop to the relentless surf. The pulse of the sea made Clett's eyes heavy. What was Rust doing here? His head nodded and jerked, and, wedged behind the steering wheel in the little car, out of the windscreen, through the snow, in the warmth, he started to dream.

"Miss, Miss", he said, pushing his hand into the air, his bare knees jammed under the tiny desk.

Out of the sound of the wind, he heard Christine's voice

"Roland, let someone else answer. Peedie Ronnie, what about you?"

Ronnie Rust sank down in his chair, gripping the needle of a pair of compasses.

"Why don't you try, Ronnie. You know the capital of Canada, don't you?"

Roland continued stretching his hand in the air, whispering:

"Miss, Miss", I know.

"I know you know, Roland. Give someone else a chance. C'mon Ronnie."

Ronnie remained silent, scratching on the surface of his desk.

"Miss, Miss", mouthed Roland, his knees scraping on the bare wood under the desk."

Christine went to Ronnie, hunched over his desk, and started to stroke his hair. The boy flinched and turned away from the teacher.

"Wee Ronnie, what is to become of you?"

"Miss, Miss, It's Ottawa, it's Ottawa"

Behind him, Roland felt the stab of the needle and he started to cry. Then another stab, repeating until Clett saw Rust peering in the windscreen at him, laughing. Clett couldn't move and Rust's laugh was a cackle, then a roar. Rust's face was replaced by Nelson's, cursing him for his incompetence.

Rust stood by the Polo, tapping his fingers on the roof, the even rhythm resonating throughout the car and in Clett's dream, maintaining the tension in his unconscious, the oscillation inescapable. Rust stared in at Clett, sleeping. The drumming was now relentless and Clett jolted awake. There was nothing out of the car window but the black sky and the snow-covered flagstones. He wiped away his tears as the pattering continued, and he looked around, realising that the sound was rain on the roof of the car. He turned his lights on; Rust's BMW had gone, leaving only the light snow falling on the dark ocean

CHAPTER TWELVE

rust

T-Block, RAF Whale Head
Tuesday 8th December 1942

Henry lifted the latest copy of *The Orkney Blast* and read the report of the dance at Lyness.

> *"Another fine evening of dancing and cavorting to music from our very own 'RAF Band'. There was Denny Young tinkling the ivories, the dashing Stan Webb putting horsehair to catgut, Jack Williams on trumpet, Billy Wiltshire on drums, and Cecil Padbury twanging his guitar. Spotted in the dancers was one of England's finest actors, Mr Bernard Miles. We requested a small recitation, and between musical numbers, he did us the honour of reciting the famous lines from The Bard:*
> > *"This story shall the good man teach his son,*
> > *And Crispin Crispian shall ne'er go by,*
> > *From this day to the ending of the world,*
> > *But we in it shall be remembered;*
> > *We few, we happy few, we band of brothers.*
> > *For he to-day that sheds his blood with me*
> > *Shall be my brother."*
>
> *Ah, stirring words indeed! Your giddy reporter, ever the man to spot a pretty girl, could not help but notice Miss Charlotte Hall, who hails from sunny Shere in Surrey. She struck a fine step a long way from home, but happy in 'Bloody Orkney!' "I just love it here. The best rations in the war!" Miss Hall was on the arm of a dashing young Lieutenant Jim Manners – lucky lieutenant if you ask me!*
> > *P.W. The dancing reporter.*

Henry had also heard about Charlotte's telegram. She had been confined to barracks for the day, so he knew it was bad news. Putting it all together, he had deduced that the telegram had informed her of a death in her family, probably back down south. However, could it be that her new beau from Lyness had been killed in action? Was there any chance? Yes, that would be perfect. In any case, he could work out an approach to Charlotte, to show her how he cared for her and her alone, to support her in her sadness.

He put down *The Orkney Blast* and looked around, enjoying his solitary nightshift. He opened the transmitter cabinet doors, exposing the thirteen-inch water-cooled power tetrode that created the energy that fed the massive aerial array outside. Across in R-Block they would be chatting and drinking tea, but Henry enjoyed his time alone under the yellow glow of the forty-watt lamps, and the flickering blue light from the transmitter cabinet. He lit a Woodbine and turned off the lights, returning to the desk, listening to the soft sounds of the gurgling, pulsing transmitter.

The valves' heaters bathed the cabinet in a warm red glow. But inside the tetrode was the dancing blue light, the effect of thirteen thousand volts tearing electrons from the cathode, translating their energy into something that would vanish in the ether in invisible waves that filled the sky. These waves sought objects that reflected the energy that was sniffed by the receivers, showing the danger in the air; to be observed by the girls on the CRTs. Girls like Charlotte, monitoring the green phosphorescence, waiting in their blue grey uniforms, waiting for the reflections in the ether to rise above the clutter, in the afterglow. Henry felt that somehow this was the connection between him and Charlotte; this magical energy that fluttered between them. Henry knew that he just had to understand this energy to find the key to Charlotte's heart.

Burgh Road Police Station, Kirkwall
Tuesday 21st December 2010

"All your Christmas shopping done, Inspector?"

Clett shook himself, squinting at the flickering lights of the artificial tree.

"Eh, no. I've been…"

The desk sergeant smiled.

"I know, sir. Mad, isn't it, just mad."

Clett looked at the desk sergeant and nodded. Outside, past the brown slush of the car park, sunshine glinted on the snow, a million shining grains mirroring the light from the momentary midday sun.

"Yes, mad."

He went to his desk and ran his fingers over the gouges on the veneer, over the sworls and circles and runes that exposed the chipboard beneath.

"Late night, sir. Getting into the Christmas spirit?"

Constable Nancie Keldie stood at Clett's desk. He stretched and yawned.

"Not exactly. I'd like to see the list of people interviewed at the Noup Head dig site in April."

"It's on the server, sir. I'll send you the link."

"Thanks, Nancie."

Clett clicked on the document containing the interviews, scrolling down until he came to an entry transcribed from Special Constable Archie Drever's notebook. He dialled the number at the bottom of the page.

"Rodger, Inspector Clett from Kirkwall Police."

"Hello."

"Rodger, this is about the account you gave to Special Constable Drever after the murder at Noup Head on 21st April."

There was a pause.

"Yes, Inspector."

"Rodger, when you were interviewed, you said that there was a local visitor to the site."

"Yes. We called him Uncle Ronnie."

"What?"

"Yes Inspector, that's what he called himself. He visited the site a few times. Great guy, always bringing stuff over for us."

"Things like drugs, Rodger?"

Rodger was silent.

"I, eh..."

"It's ok Rodger, I am not interested in the drugs, I am interested in Uncle Ronnie. What did he look like?"

"He was a kinda big guy; stocky wi' rosy cheeks."

"I see. What car did he drive?"

"A silver BMW with personalised plates."

Clett's heart was pounding.

"And how did the drugs handover work?"

"I don't know. Uncle Ronnie and Trevor discussed all that in private, usually at the Pierowall Hotel."

"So, de Vries was involved with Rust. Is that how you got the drugs?"

"It was not as if it was every night, just now and again, we would share a few spliffs that just appeared."

"Thanks Rodger, that is useful."

"No problem Inspector. Eh, about the cannabis thing?"

"Don't worry about that Rodger, but in future, be discreet."

"Thank you, Inspector."

Clett filled his chest and exhaled slowly. His chair squeaked, and he smiled, his fingertips tracing the patterns on his desk.

* * *

Ronnie Rust stopped his BMW at the steps of the Cathedral and wound down the window.

"Good morning, Jeannie. What about this snow?"

"Hello Mister Rust. I've seen naethin' like it, Mister Rust. It's that global warning that's tae blame."

"Nae doubt, Jeannie; nae doubt."

Rust drove a few yards down to the parked cars at the newsagent on the corner.

"Hello there, Tommy. Fine new car you have there?"

"Aye, Mister Rust. SUV, all-wheel drive. Just right for this weather."

"Astute buy there, Tommy, very astute."

"Mister Rust, did I hear you're standing for the council?"

"Indeed, you did, Tommy, indeed you did."

"Well, I for one am pleased you are. We need someone like you with his hands on the tiller – if you get my drift."

"Tommy, you know, I just want to do my bit."

"You'll hae your hands full dealing wi' that lot Mister Rust."

"You ken, Tommy, they are all good people trying to do a good job. I'll just be one of the team – if I'm elected."

"There's no doubt you'll get elected, Mister Rust, no doubt at all."

"That's kind of you to say, Tommy, very kind."

Rust drove further down to where Broad Street became Victoria Street, the wheels softly plashing in the slush. The snow started to fall, just the odd flake, then it lay, and built up once more. He stopped the car, stepped out and stood in front of the small shop window. The centre piece was a leather ball, smaller than a football, newly stitched and gleaming, each alternate segment half coloured black. The sign read:

'The 2010 Christmas Day Ba'. Made by Danny Harrison'

Rust saw his reflection in the window, the snow coating his hair and the shoulders of his track suit. He entered the shop.

"Fine Ba'."

"Mister Rust. Good afternoon to you. It is indeed a fine Ba'. Solid, filled wi' powdered cork – so it will float in the harbour."

"Yes, I know. May I?"

"Certainly, Mister Rust."

Rust picked up the Ba', feeling its weight.

"It's no heavy at all."

"No, but it is solid."

Rust pressed on the Ba' with his thumbs. There was no give.

"Are you playing this year, Mister Rust?"

"The Christmas Day game."

"Uppie or Doonie?"

"Country player. I'll be wi' Doon-the-Gates. Yourself?"

"I'm too old for that now, Mister Rust. I've had my day, though; nearly won, in 1975. It was gie freezing in the harbour though. Good days."

"Aye, good days."

"Will this be your first Ba', Mister Rust?"

"Aye."

"The sport of princes and fishermen. The Medicis used to play it in Florence."

Rust lifted the Ba' to his nose, breathing in the smell of polished leather, stroking the polished surface.

"Medici Princes, eh!"

* * *

Oleg Komolovsky was examining his phone, on his plate some broken crab-shells and uneaten rocket leaves. He looked up at the woman standing in front of him.

"Do you mind if I sit here?"

Komolovsky gestured to the empty seat across the table.

"Please."

"I see you have the partain salad. How is it?"

"I'm sorry. This is a crab salad."

"Partain is the Orkney word for crab."

"Ah."

The Russian closed down his phone and put it away.

"We have met, I think?"

"My name is Christine Clett."

"Ah, your husband, the policeman. We had an interesting conversation."

A waiter interrupted them. Christine scanned the menu.

"I'll have the partain and some mineral water, please."

"Certainly, madam. Anything else for yourself, sir?"

Komolovsky waved the waiter away. He looked out to the racing clouds as the snow fell.

"I am glad to have the opportunity to talk with you, Mrs Clett. Call me Oleg."

They shook hands. Christine sat straight and cleared her throat.

"You are going to support Ronnie Rust's political campaign?"

"To the point. I like that. So it is true that information travels quickly in these islands."

"There is speculation about why you are here."

"I like it here. Mister Rust is, how should I put it... he is of interest to me."

"He is an extremely dangerous man."

Christine's shoulders started to shake. As she fingered her napkin, Komolovsky gently placed his hands over hers. Christine did not move them away.

"May I call you Christine?"

Christine Clett nodded. Blushing, she recovered and put her hands on her lap. She cleared her throat.

"Oleg. That means 'Holy', doesn't it?"

"You know about Russian names?"

"I studied Russian at University. I studied in Moscow for six months. It was a long time ago."

"Really. *V'gavrit pa russki?*"

"*Nyet.... Da, Nimnogo. Kaneshna.*"

Komolovsky nibbled a forkful of rocket leaves.

"Did Mister Rust hurt you?"

"He threatened me. It was terrifying. He killed a poor peedie wee cat, and, and…"

The Russian remained silent, nodded, then spoke, quietly:

"It must have been unpleasant for you. I am sorry you had to experience such behaviour. It is not the behaviour of a gentleman. You have not told your husband?"

"No."

"I see."

The waiter brought Christine's salad. She drank a full glass of water, slowly relaxing; the only sound the clink of cutlery and soft chatter from the other people in the restaurant. Out in Scapa Flow, a flame ignited on one of the stacks on Flotta showing bright orange in the daylight. The vapour from the flame was bent by the wind, and rose, merging into the low cloud.

"Tell me, Christine, where did you go to university?"

"Glasgow."

"And you spent time in Moscow. So, you have not always lived in Orkney."

"Just to study. I couldn't wait to get back. I don't like being away."

She took a crab claw and put it in a pair of pliers and squeezed, increasing the tension until it shattered, bits of shell over the tablecloth. She tidied the mess, put the white meat on her fork, then put it down.

"There was another time, away from here, not happy."

"Roland was working in Glasgow; it was very stressful. Not good for us. My God, why am I telling you this? I hardly know you."

"Eat your food."

Christine finished her salad.

"Have you heard the story of the selkie?"

"What is a selkie?"

"A selkie is a seal. There is a story that a selkie became human, married a man, and had a family. She wanted to go back to the sea, but her husband kept her seal's coat from her until one day, she found it and went back into the water. She never returned."

Christine took a sip of water.

"Once, when things were bad, in Glasgow – Roland was under a lot of pressure – he hid my favourite coat in a wardrobe. Funny. I'm sure he hid it to stop me returning to Orkney; but look, I'm sorry. I'm doing it again, telling you terribly inappropriate personal information."

Komolovsky leaned back in his seat. "You have read Pushkin?"

Christine smiled. "It's a long time since I talked about Pushkin."

"The poem, *'Ya vas liubil'?*"

"Yes, yes. 'I loved you once'. There's a lovely irony in his use of the impersonal language; but it doesn't translate at all well into English."

"Yet, it is simple. It is a poem about lost love, and what remains."

"Yes, it is."

"What do you do, Christine?"

"I am a teacher, here in Orkney."

"You know, you have visited my country. Let me take you back there. You would love my beautiful country."

Christine looked across the table, her eyes wide. She laughed.

"What? You must be joking. I mean, we don't even know each other. How could you…"

"Why not? I could take you. Just the two of us. I show you such things."

Christine shook her head. "Mister Komolovsky… Oleg, what on earth… I could never leave Orkney. I'm a married woman."

"You could. You only have to choose. It is serious offer."

"But you don't know me. We've just met. I'm an Orkney girl."

"You are correct. But I know enough about you. I make many decisions in my life; I trust my intuitions. I trust this one. Let me take you to Russia."

Christine laughed. "This is ridiculous. I'm not going with you to Russia, Oleg."

"I think that you will consider my offer. *Poyedem so mnoy v Rossiyu.*"

"No, Oleg. *Nyet.*"

Komolovsky took a sip of his water and smiled.

* * *

"Mrs Sclater, this is Inspector Clett from Kirkwall Police Station."

There was a slight pause on the line, the sound of plates being put down.

"Young Roland; we've no seen you on Westray for a whiley noo'."

"Aye, Mrs Sclater. I'll have to come up to visit Mum and Dad's grave."

"Aye son. Knock on the door and have a cup o' tea while you're here. But Ah'm thinking ye're no jist wantin' a wee chat, though."

"Quite right, Mrs Sclater. I'd like to ask you a few questions about the statement you made to Special Constable Archie Drever back in April."

"Aye, son. Lovely boy, wee Archie Drever. I knew his folks. Da' was a teacher, you know."

Clett waited as Mrs Sclater reminisced about Archie's family.

"So son, what dae ye want tae ask me?"

"Mrs Sclater, do you know Ronnie Rust?"

"Of course, son, Mister Rust used to come here all the time. He was born over on Papay, ye ken, but silly me, of course you knew that."

"He visited Noup Head?"

"Och, aye, son. He loved my home baking. Lovely mannie. Dinny see much o' him noo, though."

"Did you ever see him talk to Trevor de Vries, the dig team leader with the leather hat?"

"Aye son, they were gie close. Thick as thieves."

"Did you see them together around the time of the murder of Dominic Byrd?"

"Can't say that I did, son. But there was a lot o' posh-looking cars around roondabout then."

"Cars like Ronnie Rust's silver BMW?"

"Couldny say, son. One car looks the same as anither tae me. But it coulda been."

"That's very helpful, Mrs Sclater. Is there anything else you remember from that night that might have occurred to you since you made your statement?"

"It's funny, son. I was jist talking to Jocky Tulloch, along by Noltland. He was just saying that on the night o' the murd… on the night o' all that unpleasantness, he saw two men talking late on. They had an argument and one got into a big car and drove off in a hurry."

"You don't say. That is very interesting. Thanks again for your help."

"Nae bother son. Say hello to that brother o' yours, young Russell."

"I will, Mrs Sclater."

* * *

"Roland. How are you? Long time no see."

"I'm fine, Archie. Do you no' miss your old job?"

"No Roland. I'm not cut out to be a Special Constable. I'm too busy wi' the farm nowadays. After the murder, I decided that enough was enough."

"That's a great pity, Archie. You have special talents."

"Thanks Roland, but that's a' behind me noo. Anyway, whit c'n I do fir ye?"

"Remember how Ronnie Rust was seen on Westray before the murder in April?"

"Aye."

"I've just heard from Mrs Sclater that Jocky Tulloch saw him arguing with Trevor de Vries on the night of the murder."

"Do you want me to talk to her?"

"No, to Jocky, at Noltland."

"Jocky Tulloch. No problem Roland, I'll let you know how I get on."

"Thanks, Archie."

* * *

"There's more on Igor, sir."

"Igor?"

"You know, The Count's Assistant, the Polish chap, Jerzy Przybylski."

Clett rolled his eyes.

"I know," said Nancie Keldie. "Juvenile isn't it, sir?"

They grinned.

"Sir, Jerzy Przybylski runs a website back home in Poland called integrita.net.pl. It is a blog and a resource for people who want to commit suicide."

"Really. Do they describe an exit kit?"

"Yes, Inspector, explicitly."
"Ok. We need another chat with Jerzy. As soon as you like."

tannin

NAAFI, RAF Whale Head
Wednesday 9th December 1942

Sergeant Jack Cameron opened a jar of butter from Isbister's farm. This jar of butter, along with the bread and bacon they brought back to Whale Head kept up relations between the locals and the servicemen and women, for whom conditions were primitive. Side by side with the staggering technical innovation represented by these massive installations, alongside all that effort and novelty, at Chain Home stations like Whale Head, people bartered for food. They put up with the crudest toilet provisions, sleeping in dormitories, sometimes carrying their own cutlery and tin cups. Cigarettes were the readiest form of currency – Woodbines, Capstans, Players. The smell of tobacco permeated every indoor space creating a constant haze, depositing a coating of yellow nicotine on every surface. People smoked while eating and working. Tea was the other commodity. The tea-break was a religiously timetabled event: at 10.15 each morning, and at 3.00 in the afternoon, everything stopped. At Whale Head there was a good supply of milk, so the strong black tea was turned into a thick brown stew, universally regarded as a tonic to fix all ills.

Cameron spread the salty butter on a thin slice of dark bread.

"Would you like a piece, Henry?"

Cameron smiled. Henry had been watching him, each spread of the knife increasing his hatred of this man, the loathing that fuelled his ire, that motivated him in the formulation of his plan.

"No thank you, sir."

"Go on, son. You gotta keep body and soul together. Hey, it's your turn to make the tea, by the way."

Henry clenched his fists and lit the burner under the tea-urn.

Cameron felt sorry for this lad, away from home and friends. He wanted to make him happier here, where it was totally dark in winter, but light in summer, where the weather was nearly always wet and windy.

Henry took another Woodbine, bent down to the flame below the urn and, with the cigarette between his lips, he watched the end ignite in the blue flame, feeling the searing heat scorch his eyebrows, enjoying the satisfying smell of burnt hair.

Harbour Street Backpackers Hostel, Kirkwall
Wednesday 22nd December 2010

Jerzy Przybylski obtained the hostel wifi code, opened the integrita.net.pl website. The inbox contained the usual ongoing queries from the near-desperate and the merely curious. Regular stuff, no surprises. He searched for a logon from Orkney and relaxed as the computer came up with the 'Not Found' response. He was relieved. If the police discovered a link, it would be awkward. He googled the website for the religious order on Papa Westray, where he found Cyd's email address. He started to type:

"Hi Cyd. Thanks for the visit…"

Jerzy stopped typing, deleted the message, and shut down the computer.

Pierowall, Westray
Wednesday 22nd December 2010

Jocky Tulloch took some cash from the bank machine, crossed the road and opened his car door.

"Jocky."

"Archie."

They shook hands.

"How about this snow?"

"Never known it to lie like this. How are your coos?"

"Och, fine. I put them in the barn."

"Aye, they'll no' be happy bein' cooped up."

"An' I'll ha'e tae clean it a' when they come oot."

They watched as the little Golden Mariana from Papa Westray

berthed at Gill Pier.

"Mind that mannie, Ronnie Rust. Did you ever see him up here?"

"Ah thought ye'd given up the police work."

"I jist answer the odd telephone call noo."

"Hmmm… Mister Rust fae the Mainland? No seen him fir a whiley. Used to see him before that terrible murder o' that young chap at Noup Head, but no since."

"Did ye ever see him talking tae anyone?"

"Aye, he wiz wi the archaeologist chap, him who looked like the mannie oot o' Raiders o' the Lost Ark."

"Trevor de Vries?"

"That was his name. He drove a Land Rover. He committed suicide, did he no'?"

"He did. Very sad. Did ye see them together on the night o' the murder?"

"Aye. I was just tellin' Jessie Sclater the other day. I suppose I should have told the police, but I don't know, what wi' the farm an' everything. They never knocked ma door."

"Can you tell me now?"

"That I can. It was the first night o' that volcanic ash business."

Jocky closed his car door and leant on the bonnet. The two men watched foot passengers disembarking from the Golden Mariana.

"It wis late, well after midnight. The moon wis bright the way it is, skyare[5]. Ah'd been at ma coos, just in yon field tae the south o' the village; an' Ah heard a really unusual ship's bell. Ah remember that. Thocht there was a scream, too. Anyway, they were standing together o'er there, ootside the Pierowall Hotel. The mannie in the hat wi' his Land Rover, wearing that leather bunnet, and Mister Rust, in his silver BMW. They didny know I wis on the other side o' the wall."

The Golden Mariana passengers were walking up Gill Pier.

"Are you sure it was Ronnie Rust?"

"Och, aye. He his that sweatshirt he wore, wi' the rude writing on it, an' jogging troosers, and ye ken, that car o' his. Mister Rust called him 'Prof'. He was going to give De Vries money, ken, for his archaeology. He kept on slapping him on the shoulder. Ye could tell that

---

[5] Skyare – Old Norse word meaning clear, bright as in moonlight.

de Vries didny like it. Mister Rust talked aboot supporting local ventures. The professor said stuff aboot financing his archeology, the need to keep young people interested."

Jocky pushed back on his car, and the vehicle moved on its springs, squeaking slightly.

"Then De Vries asked Mister Rust what he wanted in return?"

"Aye," said Archie. "Then it became interestin'. Mister Rust spoke aboot de Vries being in Mexico, having contact wi' someone called Chant, sounded like Chapo Chant. De Vries, really wisny happy. He tried to walk away, but Mister Rust stood in his way. Mister Rust said that de Vries was doing deals wi' this guy involved with a Mexican Cartel."

"What?"

"Aye, Ah ken, here in Pierowall, jist o'er there, by oor hotel, talkin' aboot Mexican Drug Cartels on the ither side o' the world. Surreal."

Jocky shook his head. A new group of passengers were stepping on to the Golden Marrianna.

"You're saying that de Vries was selling drugs in Mexico?"

"That's whit it sounded like. De Vries ran errands for this Mexican mannie, and in return he got protection to do his archaeology."

"… and Rust wanted what… to have a similar relationship to allow him to deal drugs in Orkney?"

"Ah dinny ken; I suppose so. Mister Rust said he had a unique set of talents."

"What happened then?"

"Och, de Vries took the huff. He was feart."

"…of the Mexicans?"

"Aye, well, maybe. He said he was finished wi' all that. He was very nervous, an' they were shoutin' at each other, Mister Rust saying that he had obligations, that he knew about packets that de Vries had already brought in; De Vries said all that stuff was behind him noo. He pushed his way past Mister Rust, got into the Land Rover and headed off to his camp site."

"Unbelievable. Here on Westray!"

"Aye, well…"

"And what about Rust? What did he do then?"

"He wis really unhappy. He swore and punched the wall; you know that harled wall, just o'er there."

Archie looked at the wall by the car park of the hotel. The

harled wall was roughcast, with embedded pebbles.

"He punched that wall, there?"

"Aye. Must have gie hurt. His knuckles were a' bloody. He had a cigarette and stood around fir a bit. Ah wanted tae go home, but Ah wisny wantin' tae talk tae Mister Rust, him wi' his bad mood an all. He finished his cigarette, got intae the car an' headed off, south. He nearly hit someone oot walking in the dark."

"Did you see who it was?"

"No, Archie, he wis too far away tae see."

"Jocky, that's an awful lot of detail there. How do you remember so much?"

"A conversation like that, ye jist dae. Ah should have told the police really. They really upset ma coos, ye ken."

"Aye."

* * *

"I am going in for the Christmas Day Ba' this year."

Norman Clouston looked at his boss incredulously.

"Are you sure? I mean, I see the attraction. I would like to enter myself, but I'm not eligible. How are you eligible? You're from Papay?"

"Aye, but I was born at the Balfour Hospital and...."

"Have you thought how dangerous it would be? What if someone you had put away wanted to get back at you?"

"I can look after myself."

"Do you know, I think Ronnie Rust is entering?"

"I didn't know."

"So that's not the reason you're going in for it?"

Clett looked out over the Peedie Sea. The whirls of a new fall of snow were like a murmuration of white starlings swooping, forming new patterns in the sky with each surge of wind.

"The Ba' is part of an ancient tradition. Popes in fourteenth century Florence played a ball game with the likes of Michaelangelo Buonarotti and other political and artistic figures, alongside butchers and bakers. The classic challenge of the animal and the rule of order played out in a community."

"And what? Do you think Kirkwall is like fourteenth century Florence?"

"No Norman, for goodness' sake, I'm just saying..."

"You're mad, Roland."

"But there's something else."

"What excuse is it now for your mid-life crisis?"

"My boy Sandy said he would join wi' me."

"Oh, I see. If your boy is playing with you, that changes everything."

"No Norman, I think it would be good for us."

"Aye it would be, but what does Christine think?"

Nancie Keldie came into the open-plan office.

"Sir, did you say you're going to play in The Ba'?"

"Aye Nancie, I did."

"Well I think that's great sir. You'll be a Uppie then?"

"Aye. How did you know?"

"Och sir, I have the Ba' in my blood. If there wiz ever anither Woman's Ba', I'd be the first tae sign up. My Da wiz an Uppie winner in the 1995 Christmas Day Ba'. I saw him win. I'll never forget it, it wiz jist wonderful; seein' him hoisted up by the ithers, soakin' in the freezin' water in the harbour. We were a' so proud and happy."

Clett's phone rang.

"Sir, there is a gentleman who wishes to speak to the person in charge of the investigation into the death at Sanday."

"Ok. Put him through."

Clett waited for the click in the earpiece.

"Inspector Roland Clett here. How can I help you?"

"Hi there, this is Brother Francisco. I'm from the US of A."

"Thanks for calling, Brother Francisco. What can I do for you?"

"It's ok, Inspector, call me Cyd."

"Ok, Cyd, how can I help you?"

"Well, you know, Inspector, I'm sure it is nothing, and I hate to waste your time and all…"

"That's fine Cyd, just tell me what you have to say."

"Well, as I say, it is probably nothing, really. There are two things."

"Ok, tell me your story one step at a time."

There was a pause while Cyd took a breath.

"I was at the Coop in Kirkwall, getting our weekly supplies, standing at the ATM, and an old guy was behind me. He followed me around the supermarket and stood behind me in the checkout queue."

"If I could interrupt for a moment, Cyd, when was this?"

"23rd November, late morning, about eleven am."

"Thank you. Please continue."

"Sure. Well, I was walking out of the supermarket and he chatted, passing the time of day, talking about the weather and such like."

Clett scribbled as Cyd spoke.

"Well, this old guy, he moved slowly. He had, like arthritic hands, and a bad limp. He seemed to be in constant pain."

Clett gestured for the others in the office to be silent.

"Really."

"Yes. He asked about our order. He was very interested in our take on redemption. We get that a lot, you know; people stopping us in the streets, asking advice on sin, the afterlife and so on."

"I'm sure you do."

"Anyway, I gave him our standard script, you know, that prayer is the only way to redemption. Blah, blah."

"You seem a little blasé about your calling, Brother."

"Do not misunderstand me, Inspector. I am a profound believer in the tenets of our order, but I am well aware that these beliefs are, perhaps, a little esoteric for many people, so I have a potted version for when I am stopped outside supermarkets."

"I see. Please carry on."

"Well, I was troubled by this old guy. He had odd ideas about sin. I got the distinct impression that he had sinned greatly in his past life, that he wanted some kind of salvation. He said he was going to die. I tried to be sympathetic, but he would not allow me to comfort him. He wanted very specific answers, which I could not give him. I got the distinct impression that he was going to kill himself."

"What did you say to him?"

"I said I would pray for him."

"And his response?"

"He got angry and swore at me. He said he was answerable for his own sins. I repeated that he would only gain salvation through the power of prayer."

"Did you get his name?"

"No, but I have been worrying about him since. Could I have done more?"

"Cyd, you must know from your own experience these are often unsatisfactory conversations. The fact that you were there and listened to him would have been kindness enough."

"But that is the point, Inspector. I am not sure that I did listen to him."

"I'm sorry, Cyd. It sounds to me like you did the right thing. From our point of view, this is useful information. Was there a second story?"

"Yes, absolutely, Inspector. All this talk about suicide and assisted killing got me to thinking about an online theological debate that I have been having with a guy in Poland who runs a website that purports to support people who wish to do away with themselves."

"Do you know this man's name?"

"Sure; Jerzy Przybylski."

Clett took a deep breath. "This is very helpful. Please continue, Cyd."

"Well, Jerzy disagreed with us quite forcefully. He actually came to visit me at our monastery, to discuss it."

"When did this happen?"

"The day before yesterday."

"Really."

"Yes. I heard about the man they found on Sanday. It sounded to me like there was a connection. Do you think there is a connection, Inspector?"

"I'm afraid I couldn't say at the moment, Cyd. However, be assured that this conversation is being treated extremely seriously."

"That's good enough for me, Inspector."

* * *

The Caledonian Mercury, Edinburgh,
Thursday 15th December 1748 No 4397
Extract of a letter from Orkney, Dec 8th

I should wish to respond to Dr Sinclair in his letter of the 6th inst. He wishes to stop those who play the game of the ball in the streets of Kirkwall. He states that these individuals are merely feral, that they have no concern for civilisation and the rule of our laws or the protection of property, and that they are merely animals.

I would not disagree with these points, but I would object to the use of the word 'merely'. This game is played all over the world. I have seen it on the streets of Firenze where the finest nobles engage with their tailors and their tanners in the game of the ball in their fine streets. The game of the ball represents an engagement with these undeniable sides of our human nature. It celebrates our past and allows those of us who choose to observe how the film of civilisation is so fragile, so precious that we must nurture it as one does a delicate flower. We let the spurious leafy growths thrive in order to see the flower blossom. The nature of the flower is to enjoy a balance between the less lovely leaf and its profound beauty. So goes it with our human activities. We must allow some room for the rude part of us be exorcised, and in doing so, we can otherwise savour the everyday joys of peace and harmony that is the fruit of civilised society.
Archibald Clett of Canmore

* * *

Clett sat in his study looking out at the snow, still drifting, obscuring the features in the Clett's garden. A light grey fog hung in the air. Clett called as he heard the door open. He helped carry bags of shopping to the kitchen. Christine removed food from the bags and put it in the fridge.

"You've been a while."

"Have I?"

"Where have you been?"

"Where does it look like I have been?"

"The Supermarket? For all that time?"

Christine stopped, examining a packet of pasta.

"Do you have any idea what happens in my life, in my work, in what I am interested in, in what I think?"

"What? Where is this coming from?"

Cristine shook her head and carried on unpacking.

"No, really Christine, what is it? What's wrong?"

"I just need a cup of tea."

Clett quickly filled the kettle and put a tea-bag into a mug. He squeezed Christine's waist, and she turned away.

"I'm sorry Roland, I'm not sure I can take much more of this?"

"What? Christ, what has happened?"

"See, you've not even noticed how I have been feeling."

"I've been a bit pre-occupied."

"Maybe even self-obsessed?"

"Wow."

The kettle rumbled. Christine looked out the window as Clett slowly took a carton of milk from the fridge.

"Have I really been ignoring you so much?"

"Work it out, Roland."

"God. I'm so sorry, Christine. I'll make it up to you. What do you want me to do?"

"You see. There it is; In the old days, you would never have had to ask me a question like that."

He stood in the middle of the kitchen, milk carton in hand as the kettle came to the boil.

"I don't know what to say."

"Why don't you tell me something about you, Roland? You always have something to say about yourself, *your* investigations, *your* problems, *your* obsession with Rust."

"Christine. I'm so sorry. I didn't realise…"

"No Roland, you never do."

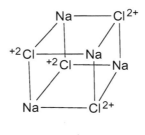

salt

T-Block, RAF Whale Head
Thursday 10th December 1942

"What will you do after the war?"

Jack Cameron offered Henry a Camel.

"I smoke Woodbine."

"I know you do; have one of mine."

"No thank you, sir."

The sergeant put away the Camels and took his pipe from his pocket. He tapped the old tobacco into an ashtray, blew the pipe clear and pinched a fresh filling from a leather pouch. Out of the corner of his eye, Henry watched with clenched teeth. The older man lit the tobacco, sucking noisily, pressing the glowing embers down with his thumb, immune to the burn. Cameron caught Henry looking at him.

"So, Private?"

"So, what, sir?"

"So, what *will* you do after the war?"

"The war will never end. I don't want it to end."

"Don't you want to go home to your family, your friends; to get a normal job, to live life?"

Henry grunted.

"I like it here."

"Here in Orkney, with the weather and the cold and the uncomfortable beds?"

"I like it here."

Henry was aware of the pulsing transmitter, the hiccupping

water pump. He could feel its warmth from eight feet away.

"You like it in Orkney."

"I like it in T-Block."

"You don't say. You are truly an interesting young man."

Cameron re-lit his pipe, the pungent odour drifting across the room. Henry felt his whole body physically pulse in synchronisation with the transmitter. At the same time, he fumed, inwardly raging at the Canadian's very presence. He had let himself down; Cameron now had knowledge of Henry's private thoughts. This man, more and more, represented all the problems in his life, which boiled down to one fundamental thing: he was the cause of his thwarted love for Charlotte. If it had not been for Cameron, Henry could have had a chance of happiness with Charlotte. He was the focus of Henry's ire. A world without that man would be a good world for Henry Long. Henry looked around. He could do it now: there, the revolver in the locked drawer. But how would he get to it? Cameron was a big man; he thought about the heavy tools in the workshop: it would be an easy matter to take a large spanner...

With these thoughts, he stared at Cameron, not six feet from him, smiling that ingratiating smile. Henry breathed in the smell of his foreign tobacco and found himself exhilarated with the logic and coherence of the decision crystallising in his mind. The prospect of dispatching this man seemed so sensible — like when you decide to do something and there is no alternative course of action that makes any sense — but Henry had to wait. He had to be methodical, choose a method whereby he would not be found out. He took a sheet of paper and made a list: revolver, spanner, strangulation.

He considered the earth wand hanging by the transmitter, lifting it, feeling its weight. But no, it was too flimsy. The soft copper would bend and be ineffective. Henry bent down and examined it in more detail. He followed the lead that attached it to the earthing point, fingering the nut.

"The earth wand is your friend. Use it
regularly, and you will be in no danger."

Sergeant Cameron looked up from his pipe, sucking in the warm tobacco smoke.

"Is there a problem, Henry?"

Henry seethed at the sound of his name coming from that mouth.

"Just checking the earth wand bolts are secure, sir."
"Good man."

* * *

Sent today at 11:10:22
From: Irene Seath
Subject: ORK/2010/12/14/Lopness SPSA SOCO Daily Update
To: Roland Clett (Insp); Margaret McPhee (CI)
Cc: Norman Clouston (Sgt.); Sanja Dilpit (SOCO)

Good evening Inspector. See below daily update as per SLO. Para 3.13:
Para 2.12
The as-yet unnamed individual is thought to be a recluse who may have lived approximately one mile from the locus. No DNA or dental records are available. Ongoing attempts at identification are not currently possible by forensic methodology.
(At the moment, local police enquiries are ongoing.)
Para 5.2
Following an observation from local police (PC Norman Clouston) of a sick sheep, the animal was seen by local veterinary surgeon, (Dr Thomas Seaton). The animal was sedated, and a plastic bag removed from its oesophagus. It is fortunate that the bag had not been digested as traces of ether have been identified on the surface of the plastic. Significant erosion of the bag was observed due to corrosive contact with the ether. It would seem to follow that this bag is likely to have been used by the deceased for inhalation of the ether. This bag has been retained in the evidence tray and will be allocated a reference at the end of the investigation.
Para 11.3
The hard disc of the computer used by the deceased was erased by means of a Unix script that wrote the entire hard disc with zeroes, thus ensuring that no data can be recovered. Also, IP addresses of routers and

firewalls have constantly been changing using a unique process that has left no trace of web activity. A search of social media sites shows no accounts associated with the deceased. This investigation is ongoing.

Results to be appended to ORK/2010/12/14/Lopness (Full report on secure drive).

Once again, another update tomorrow at 11.00 as per SPSA SLA (2008). As always, please get in touch if any queries arise.

Regards

Irene Seath (SOCO) 07222 176687

Sanja Dilpit. (SOCO) 07222 176688

ps For info, Inspector, SOCO staff will be vacating site tomorrow for Christmas, but Sanja and I have decided to stay over to watch The Ba' on Christmas Day. We heard you were going to be taking part :)

* * *

Children's Hearing Centre, Watergate, Kirkwall
Thursday 23rd December 2010

Clett supported Geraldine's arm as they entered the Children's Hearing room, high with a corniced ceiling. She was wearing clean clothes and had made an attempt at applying make-up but could not hide her red and swollen eyes. She sat close to Raymond as they held hands, whispering little things in each other's ear; comforting each other. The boy smiled nervously as people in the room introduced themselves. The chair of the panel, a pleasant woman in her forties went through the procedures, and the social worker sympathetically laid out her reasons for wishing Raymond to be taken into care: Geraldine was not capable of looking after herself and could not prioritise the needs of her son; he needed stability and the consistency of care that she was not able to give him. Geraldine started crying and Raymond got her a tissue from a box on the table. He gave her a hug. The panel were discussing accommodation options when Clett spoke up.

"Madame chair, I would like to offer a character reference for Ms Work."

"Go ahead, Inspector."

"Ms Work is a young woman who has had a difficult start; As you will probably see from the reports, both her parents died in a house fire some years ago. Last year she managed to turn her life around, holding down a responsible job, at the same time as caring for her son as a single parent. It was only after a violent assault that she had significant difficulties. I would suggest these difficulties may be down to post traumatic stress disorder that has not been addressed."

"I agree," said the social worker.

One of the panel members, a young man with a large beard, responded: "Yes Inspector, we can understand that this is the unfortunate sequence of events that has brought us here today. I would encourage Ms Work to seek counselling."

The social worker nodded. "I can set this up."

The panel member continued. "The role of the panel is to make a decision that addresses the welfare needs of Raymond."

Raymond whispered in his mother's ear, and she answered:

"Yes, Raymond these people will decide what is best for you."

The chair spoke to Raymond.

"Raymond, would you like to say something to the panel? You could speak to us on your own if you like."

He looked nervously at Geraldine.

"I just want to go home with Mummy."

"Do you feel safe with your mummy?"

"My mummy never hurt me. Never, she's my mummy."

"Yes, Raymond, we can see that you love each other very much."

The chair scanned a page of the report in front of her.

"Raymond, what is your favourite food that your mummy cooks?"

Raymond looked at Geraldine, who was blushing.

"My mummy cooks for me all the time. My mummy is a brilliant cook. She is going to cook on television."

Geraldine wiped away a tear,

"It's all right, Raymond…"

She squeezed her son's hand.

"I have read what you have in your reports. It is all true. I should have been a better mother to my son."

"Thank you, Ms Work. That is very helpful."

Clett coughed.

"Excuse me, may I ask if consideration has been made to allow Raymond to stay with his Nan on Shapinsay? Ms Work might be able to see him there."

"That is my recommendation," said the social worker.

The hearing discussed the option and made their deliberation. Raymond was to live with his Nan in Shapinsay under a supervision order and he was to see his mum twice a week. As they left the room, Geraldine turned to Clett.

"Thank you so much Inspector. Now I can have Christmas with Raymond and my mum."

"That's all right, Geraldine. You know now that you have to get yourself on your feet again. Do what social work say, and soon you will be able to get Raymond back again. Merry Christmas."

He left the little group hugging in the corridor and headed down Tankerness Lane towards Burgh Road Police Station.

* * *

Clett pressed the record button on the interview recorder.

"Interview commenced, Friday 24th December 2010, Kirkwall Police Station. Present: Inspector Roland Clett, Constable Nancie Keldie, and the interviewee Jerzy Przybylski."

"Let's talk about your website, Jerzy: www.integrita.net.pl."

"Certainly, Inspector."

Nancie Keldie turned a laptop round to face Jerzy.

"That is my website."

Nancie clicked on a link. Clett nodded.

"This is a description of an exit kit."

"Yes, Inspector."

"A method of killing oneself…"

"Yes Inspector, a method that is… dignified. I think that it is also important to observe… what is the word, yes, to observe context. As I have told you, I was a priest. I am no longer priest, but I believe in importance of ritual."

"But you admit that your website clearly describes how to commit suicide."

"You have the evidence in front of you, Inspector, but you are missing my point."

"No, Jerzy. I hate to say it, but we have strong circumstantial evidence linking you to the death of the man found at Lopness, on Sanday."

"Indulge me, Inspector. I do not merely tell people how to – how do you say here – 'to do away with yourself'. I recognise that these people are in – what is the word, yes, a turmoil, but they must see through this, they must treat their own lives with integrity. They are not just machines that they are turning off. You would be surprised how many people I talk to that are so desperate that they lose sight of the value of their own lives, all that experience, all that love, yes, all that love, in all its forms just evaporating. They must reflect and celebrate that reflection in a symbolic ritual act."

"You mean like candles, like bowls of salt?"

"Perhaps."

"Did anyone from Orkney log on to your website?"

"I cannot say."

Nancie Keldie interrupted. "Sir, I've looked through the forums on the integrita website and there's no obvious indication of an English speaker from Orkney."

"Do we know if the dead man speak any other languages?"

"Don't know, Inspector, but we are waiting on another report from Irene and Sanja. They may have an ID."

"Jerzy, once again, I will ask you straight. Did you have anything to do with the death at Lopness?"

"Inspector, many people look at my website. Not everyone will engage directly. Some people don't use their real names; I have no way of knowing. I am very sorry I cannot help you more."

"Jerzy, I am going to want to talk to you again, very soon. I have to tell you, this is not looking good. We absolutely need clarification on your actions. Just tell us what you know."

Jerzy Przybylski smiled, a peaceful smile that Clett could not ignore. Clett hesitated and his shoulders dropped as he closed the case folder.

"Try to stay calm Inspector. It will all be over soon."

He touched Clett softly on the shoulder, just once.

* * *

As Clett lifted his phone, it buzzed. It was Christine. He paused, then pressed 'end call'. He searched in his contacts for Tony Nelson, Glasgow

CID and tapped the call button. He really did not want to have this conversation. The number rang at the other end and Clett felt a sense of relief. The phone continued to ring. Clett held his finger over the end call button, about to hang up when he heard the familiar unpleasant voice at the other end of the phone.

"*Inspector* Roland Clett, as I live and breathe."

"Hello Tony, how are you?"

"You see it all, my friend, you see it all. What can I do you for?"

"We're reviewing the circumstances of the murder of Dominic Byrd at Noup Head in April. Some evidence has come to light that changes things, and I would like to hear your perspective, that is, if you have a minute."

"Always happy to assist our friends in the north. What have you got?"

"Trevor de Vries…"

"The dig team leader who hanged himself in custody?"

"Yes. We now have financial records that show large sums of money coming into his account during the time he spent running tours of archaeological digs in Mexico. We received information from Norfolk CID that substantiated our theory that he was involved in low-level cartel activity, bringing drugs into the UK disguised as archaeological samples. It appears that he did errands for a cartel member in exchange for funds to run his archaeological tours and digs. Looks like he was working for a man called El Chapo Sant."

"Fuck me!"

"Yes, he does appear to have been in tow with serious people."

"That's a fucking understatement, Inspector. Chapo is a world player. He has his own army. Lives in a stockaded villa in the mountains. That means that our boy, de Vries was operating at a very high level indeed."

"I'm not so sure. It looks like he got out when things became too dangerous."

"So he came to Orkney, a world away from Mexican drug cartels."

"That it is."

"Do you think the Mexicans had a hand in his death?"

"There's no evidence to suggest that. The simple answer is the one that came out in court. Dominic Byrd was killed in a pathetic motiveless murder. There is no information to suggest otherwise."

"Hmm… but you're going to tell me more."

"Yes, Tony. Do you remember Ronnie Rust?"

"I most certainly do. Good man. Bit rough around the edges, but you know where you stand with him."

Clett paused and clenched and unclenched his fist. "Indeed. It looks like he met with de Vries prior to the murder at Noup Head. Rust knew about his Mexican connections and wanted to set up some kind of arrangement to route drugs into and through Orkney. They had a meeting on the night of the murder and fell out. De Vries was witnessed walking away, presumably unwilling to get into all that stuff again."

"Interesting. That might work strategically, but I can't see Mister Rust becoming involved like that. I know he has history, but he's a reformed man. I met him at an anti-corruption seminar in Glasgow last month."

"What? Ronnie Rust?"

"Aye, he's standing for Orkney Islands Council…"

"I know that, but you met him?"

"Aye just for a chat. Your name came up in the conversation."

Clett's heart was pounding.

* * *

"Ok, everyone, I've received the daily SOCO update from Sanja and Irene, as well as a report from Erik Skea on Sanday. Erik has information on The Count'. No name yet, but it is thought that he was a recluse who lived about a mile from Lopness, where the body was found. Locals knew nothing about him. He lived alone in a two-room house filled with old newspapers and milk cartons. One room was full of bin bags. In the other, between piles of newspapers, was a path to a desk laden with computers and radio equipment. He was a radio amateur with very expensive looking gear. Receipts for local food supplies were found on his desk dated the 12th and 13th of December. There is a ticket for a return ferry trip between Houton and Hoy on 12th."

"Any DNA or other data?"

"This gentleman has no recorded DNA data, or any other data for that matter. We have a name, but no other information. He received a pension in the post which he banked and cashed immediately. The account is in his own name. Apart from that there is no information on this person. Digitally speaking, evidentially speaking, he is a ghost."

"He must have a National Insurance Number"

"We are communicating with the Department of Work and Pensions, and we hope to have a response soon."

"So we do it the old fashioned way?"

"We do it the old-fashioned way."

"What about the radio amateur connection?"

Clett scanned his briefing note.

"He operated using the callsign G3FJG, first registered in1946."

Nancie Keldie coughed. "Sir, maybe I could call my Uncle Joe at the Kirkwall Wireless museum. We might get something about his radio ham activity. Not optimistic about getting anything useful though. All their logged information is about signal strengths and other callsigns communicated with; weather, sunspot activity. That kind of thing."

"Thanks, Nancie. See how you get on."

Clett scanned Erik Skea's email on his phone:

"It looks like no one knew this man. He lived alone and was never seen by the locals – except on his weekly walk to the shop to buy basics. Looks like he was something of a hermit. They say he walked with a limp."

"Sanja and Irene's report mentioned a pebble in his shoe."

Clett shuffled some papers on his desk.

"Thanks to Norman's suggestion, Sanja and Irene now say that it is highly likely that a sheep ate the plastic bag that was used to contain and inhale the ether."

"What about the contents of his computer?"

"They have been unable to retrieve anything from it."

"I thought that they could re-create deleted files from fragments."

"Not in this case. He wiped the computer with zeroes, over-writing the whole hard disc. He knew what he was doing."

"What about the receipts, all with the same date, 12th December this year, two weeks ago, also the Houton to Lyness ferry ticket? Could someone arrange interviews with anyone who was on that ferry that day?

People looked at their watches.

"Ok, it's the 24th tomorrow. Let's try to tidy this up before

Christmas Day."

Outside, another layer of snow fell on the piles of snow by the sides of the parked cars in the Burgh Road car park. Early evening traffic rumbled quietly along the road, slowly following cones of light from their headlights, illuminating the swirling snow.

"Good night everyone."

Clett's phone buzzed, showing three missed calls from Christine. He called back and was connected straight to her voicemail. He didn't leave a message.

* * *

Clett peered through the windscreen wipers as he drove west towards Orphir. As he passed the Foveran restaurant, he saw Christine's car; across the car park, two black SUVs belonging to Oleg Komolovsky. His heart pounding, he pulled in and went inside. As he wiped the snow from his bare head, he scanned the tables. Christine and Komolovsky were sitting together, laughing. Clett sucked at the seeming thin air, his vision swimming.

CHAPTER FIFTEEN

lithium

RAF Whale Head
Friday 11th December 1942

In Henry's mind there was a profound link between T-Block and R-Block. It went beyond the electrical connections between transmitter and the receiver. You could see it in the blue light of the ions inside the valve, and the CRT screen, its dancing pulses representing the reflections of objects in the sky. He was utterly convinced that these connections bound him and Charlotte together in a way he was still trying to understand. More than pleasantries, it went beyond the normal veneer that dictated everyday social interaction. Some people might call it love. Henry would associate his own feelings for Charlotte, his beautiful obsession with her, these things that were beyond mere words, it seemed embedded in their existence, transmitted between their bodies by means of the ether. If only Henry could communicate the nature of their shared destiny, to move on from his humiliation. It irritated Henry that he had sent the poem to Charlotte. He had acted too soon; he needed a new approach, to get over the recent awkwardness, to prove that their connection was present through the manifest force of nature. More research was what was required. But there was another obstacle to this plan. Cameron was in the way of any possibility of having a meaningful discussion with Charlotte about the nature of their relationship, bound by the elements of nature, the aurora that linked them, the plasma via the ether, to the phosphorescence on her CRT.

Henry took the dog-eared sheet of paper from his shirt pocket. It was now full of little arrows linking words together; the matrix overwritten with question marks and crossings out. But there, in the middle of the page, circled, underlined was: 'Earth Wand'.

Henry took a spanner from the T-Block workshop, and stood in front of the pulsing, throbbing organism that was the transmitter, swelling and retreating in sympathy with his heartbeat. He knelt down and, with the spanner, he unscrewed the earth wand connector, disconnecting it from the electrical ground, so that it could no longer discharge the thousands of volts on the transmitter's hotspots.

Out in the Isbisters' doocot, in the clear, brief, sunshine, doos fluttered and coo'd in their stone nests. In their field, the soft cattle moved between the barbed wire fences that marked out the territory of war on these islands.

Finstown
Thursday 23ʳᵈ December 2010

Christine tossed her car keys on the coffee table. Clett was washing dishes.

"You shouldn't have bothered with that."

Clett remained silent.

"Bad day at work?"

Clett knocked over a mug that smashed on the floor. He closed his eyes.

"That was from our holiday in Yosemite."

"I saw you."

"Sorry?"

"With Komolovski."

Clett picked up the pieces and put them in the dustbin.

"You were getting on well."

Christine put her fingertips together, bending the palms of her hands away from each other.

"How long has this been going on?"

"I, eh,. We've… a few times."

"Why, Christine?"

"You know why, Roland. Have you any idea how hard it is dealing with your moods, your unpredictability? Every day… you know, I can taste it in this house, I can taste it in our home."

"It's just work, Christine. It's important."

"You get so involved; there is no separation between your work and your life. Your work is now embedded in this home."

"It is just a busy period. It will pass."

"No, Roland. You can't deal with your feelings of persecution. You should go back on the medication. We've been here before. I can't go through it all again."

"So. This is the reason you are seeing a Russian gangster."

"He's not a gangster. It's just nice speaking Russian after all these years. For your information, I'm actually getting him to put a stop to Ronnie Rust's ambitions. In a funny way, it is to help you."

"What? You're sleeping with him to help me. Jesus Christ, Christine!"

"I'm not sleeping with him. Oh God, this is coming out all wrong."

Houton pier, boarding the ferry to Lyness, Hoy
Sunday 12th December 2010

Janie Shearer fixed her make-up in the mirror as Ronnie Rust manoeuvred the BMW, rumbling up the ramp to the MV Hoy Head, positioning the vehicle at the front of the queue. He locked the car and they climbed the steps to the upper deck by the funnel, out of the wind, looking east, inhaling the sea air.

"Mister Rust?"

Rust was engulfed by the panorama, the snow-covered landscape and the two blues of the sky and Scapa Flow, split by the horizon. Over the water, swirls of little blizzards formed changing shapes that dissolved in the cold air.

"Mister Rust?"

Janie touched his arm of his tracksuit and Rust recoiled, jolting away from her.

"I'm sorry Mister Rust. I didn't realise."

Rust took a deep breath; hesitantly placing his hand on Janie's.

"It's ok, Janie. It's just that I don't like people touching me. I'm not used to it, you see."

"Mister Rust, I'm so sorry. You poor man, you mean no one has ever given you…"

Janie reached over to him once more. Again, Rust withdrew. He inhaled: "Janie, you are a lovely girl; I appreciate your affection, I just can't do physical contact."

Janie shifted away from Rust and sat upright.

"Ok, speaking in my new role as your political advisor, I think this might be a problem. People will want to shake your hand."

"I know, Janie. This is the area I need you to address. Shaking hands is ok, but touching; no. And just so as we are clear, absolutely no hugging. That makes me want to be physically sick."

"Don't worry, Mister Rust. I can fix this."

The vessel left the little harbour at Houton for Flotta and Lyness as the purser made the safety announcements over the loudspeaker. Rust and Janie Shearer descended to the lounge and made themselves comfortable.

The passenger lounge of the MV Hoy Head was warm. A couple sat with a small dog between their legs. An old man perched in the corner looking uncomfortable, his shirt buttoned to the neck, holding on to a walking stick propped between his knees. Rust sat next to him.

"Good morning to you, sir."

The man grumbled. Rust continued.

"Fine crossing today, is it not?"

The older man grunted.

"They say there's more snow on the way."

He raised an eyebrow but stayed silent. Rust persisted:

"You're not from Hoy?"

The man looked at the floor. Rust went to the drinks dispenser and poured two teas. He put sugar in one and returned. He handed one to the man who took it, warming his hands on the cardboard cup. He sniffed it.

"It's got sugar."

Rust took a drink from his own cup and the old man blew and sipped at the hot liquid.

"How did you know I took sugar?"

The ferry passed The Barrel of Butter on the port side. Across the floor, Janie Shearer glanced at the two men as she flicked through a magazine.

"My name is Ronnie Rust."

"How do you do, Mister Rust?"

They shook hands, Rust gently enclosing the old man's delicate, spindly fingers in his.

"I'm standing for Councillor in South Ronaldsay."

The man nodded, sipping his tea.

"You are on the wrong ferry, Mister Rust."

Rust grinned. "I've never been to Hoy; I decided to acquaint myself with the island. Do you know Hoy?"

"I spent a little time here during the war."

"So, you will have seen many changes."

The man nodded; Rust continued.

"Were you stationed there?"

"No, Sanday."

"So you say. What did you do on Sanday?"

"Radar."

"On Sanday?"

"Yes."

"I thought Netherbutton was the only radar station during the war."

"There were others, at Deerness, Crustan, out at Birsay. I worked at Whale Head, on Sanday. It was bombed."

"I didn't know that."

The ferry rose over a swell.

"People died."

"I'm sure they did; and you are here?"

"So it would seem."

The man grimaced as he moved. He scratched under his collar. Rust took a long drink from his cup. "Will you visit the cemetery?"

There followed a period where there was no conversation. People read or slept. A child went to the little dog lying at the couple's feet and clapped it, chucking it under the chin. The purser came around checking everyone's tickets, unsmiling. At his heel was a large black Labrador that followed him around the cabin. The larger dog looked at the lapdog and growled, sending it scuttling behind its owners' legs. Everyone eyes were on the black dog as it followed the purser, stopping, moving in step with him. The purser didn't invite conversation, his authority clear to everyone, and every passenger handed over their ticket without question. He scanned the cabin before leaving to go out on to the deck. As he did so, the black dog turned, growling. The little dog cowered under the seat as the couple patted its head.

Rust took the empty cups and dropped them in a bin and returned. The old man gestured for Rust to come close.

"There was a girl…"

Rust moved around to face the older man.

"I was responsible for her death. And a man too, but he didn't matter."

"During the bombing?"

The man nodded.

Outside, unseen in the windowless cabin, seagulls called, hovering in the wake of the vessel. Out on the deck, the Labrador barked, jumping at the birds, the sound of its bark lost in the wind.

"And you have lived with this all these years?"

The old man looked into Rust's eyes.

"A terrible thing, a terrible thing."

The old man stared at the floor.

"Sometimes...sometimes..."

Rust spoke, just loud enough to be heard over the call of seagulls and the engine noise and the sea. In the warm cabin, he sat closer.

"Have you ever thought that...?"

"Often."

"How?"

The man looked around the cabin and back at Rust; speaking softly, just audible above the engine noise.

"I found this site, on the internet, you know."

Rust cupped his ear to hear.

"My friend runs it; Jerzy, in Krakow, in Poland."

The man grimaced in pain as he pulled at the neck of his shirt. "I've ordered the ether. It's in the kitchen cupboard."

"But you can't do it?"

"I'm a coward."

"You can remain strong. How would you do it?"

"I don't know. Jerzy said that we should die for the sins of others, not for our own sins."

"Really? I would like to meet your friend Jerzy."

As the ferry docked at Flotta, in the lounge people shuffled about. Rust and the man remained in the same place. Janie Shearer watched from over her magazine. The couple continued to read their books and occasionally patted their still whimpering lapdog.

"You need a story to tell about your death. Where would you do it, what time of day, that kind of thing?"

The old man was now alert, animated, face on to his questioner.

"Mister Rust, you said your name was?"

"Call me Ronnie."

"You have a way of speaking. You are like my friend Jerzy in some ways. I can say these things."

"People are frightened to talk about death."

"Yes."

The ferry reversed out of Flotta harbour, continuing on its way to Hoy. Janie Shearer watched out of the corner of her eye. She smiled as the old man took a hold of Rust's hand.

"Mister Rust, sometimes, at home, I wear my shroud. I would like to die in T-Block."

"T-Block?"

"I was happy there."

Rust stayed silent.

The old man recognised familiar old sounds, of the gurgling of the pumps and the ship's generator.

"I would just go there, breathe in my ether and that would be that."

"How would you...?"

"A plastic bag. Easy."

"Of course."

Rust turned his head to the floor, smiling benignly. He looked up again at the man.

"Why don't you just do it?"

"I need permission."

The ferry was slowing and coming to the pier at Lyness. People were queuing to get to their cars. Janie Shearer rose and nodded to Rust, who nodded back. He stared at the old man.

"What is your name?"

"I am called Henry Long."

Rust clasped the man's hand in his and looked right into his eyes, seeing the proximity of a death.

"Henry Long, I give you permission. I give you permission to die."

Henry started to weep. He nodded.

"Thank you, Mister Rust. You have made me a happy man."

He shook Rust's hand vigorously.

"Thank you. Thank you, thank you, sir."

Rust smiled.

"It has been a privilege talking to you, Henry Long."

"You don't know what a burden you have lifted from me."

Rust shook Henry's hand in both of his and helped him to his feet, and up the steps to the deck. The purser and his dog glowered at the disembarking passengers Henry used his stick to step gingerly off the ferry on to the pier and slowly walked on, towards the old oil tanks. Rust and Shearer drove past in Rust's BMW. Rust opened his window.

"Have a good journey, Henry Long."

* * *

Henry passed through the group of old Second World War buildings, now quiet, unrecognisable from the old days, nearly seventy years before, when thirty-five thousand servicemen and women bustled around. He passed one of the old oil tanks, now converted into a museum, echoing with the thuds and booms and squeals as children played and yelled inside.

He turned right out of Lyness and headed up the hill, stumbling slowly with his stick and the pain in his hips and knees. Today it took an hour to reach the cemetery. He stopped several times for breath, taking in the view to the north over the Flow. On its return journey to Houton, the MV Hoy Head was now passing the far side of Cava with The Barrel of Butter on its starboard side. As he opened the cemetery gate, the sun came out, lighting up the hundreds of gleaming white monuments against the bright blinding snow that covered the manicured grass beneath. The headstones were grouped by ship, or location, or nationality; mostly British servicemen and women who lost their lives in a war a lifetime ago. Henry stooped to lessen the jabbing pain of the arthritis in his hip and back. His stick kept sinking in the snow, useless. Staggering, and exhausted, he shut his eyes to the white light on the headstones and stumbled across the large plot to the space he had visited every year for the last sixty-eight years. Henry held on to the headstone as he very slowly knelt down on the wet snow. He rested his hand on the granite that was chill to the touch.

After a few minutes, he stood to leave, grunting with the pain in his knees and hips. He didn't read the adjacent headstone. He knew what it said:

carbon

RAF Whale Head
Saturday 12th December 1942

"New raid. Hostile-Three-Seven, Queen Edward four zero niner niner, north-west, up to fife aircraft, twenty thousand feet."

At Dollarbeg Operations Room, under a cloud of cigarette smoke, the young women around the chart table became more animated, responding to the information, placing their tokens on the grid to the south-west of Orkney.

"Squadron of German bombers on direct heading to Scapa Flow. Imminent."

All around Scapa Flow searchlights splashed sparks, crackling as their carbon arc elements came in contact. They scanned the night sky, illuminating barrage balloons and clouds, reflecting their light back down on to the ships below. The Chain Home Radio Direction Finding stations at Netherbutton and Whale Head relayed information of hidden threat to the operators at the Filter Room in Kirkwall, and on to the Operations Room at Dollarbeg. Every second, the giant towers broadcasting thousands of pulses of radio waves into the ether, awaiting their reflections from enemy aircraft. Thus, the defence gunners and blimps could be ready to defend the Royal Fleet from attack.

The Station Commander opened the large metal door of R-Block, entering the warm receiver room with its haze of cigarette smoke, the buzz of equipment and comms chat. Charlotte was sitting at the CRT. Short commands were delivered to the telephonists across the room, relaying the information to Dollarbeg. He looked over Charlotte's shoulder at her screen, observing the patterns of green phosphorescence.

"Are you sure it's not clutter? Looks like migrating birds to me."

Charlotte glanced at the station commander and focussed on her CRT. She spoke sharply:

"Negative sir, significant beating on the signal, consistent velocity, bearing at average speed 220 knots. Suspect four or five hostiles, probably Heinkels. Height estimated at 20,000 feet, descending."

Outside, the rising sound of the air-raid klaxon filled the sky and flocks of birds rose up into the sky.

Charlotte paused and barked again at the telephone operator:

"Incoming range approximately eighty miles."

As she reached for the gonio to adjust the line of shoot, Charlotte watched in horror as her screen died, the targets no longer visible, just the glow from the fading phosphor.

In T-Block, Henry held his breath, his cigarette held in mid-air as the shocking sound of the diminishing pitch of the slowing transmitter fans, the fading glow of the valves, signified the dying of the transmitter. He stood alone, transfixed, in front of the silent transmitter. The valves became quiescent, their heaters emitted no glow. He checked – the anode voltage had been correct, but no output was transmitted, no energy was being radiated into the air; consequently, the operators could not determine whether there were targets in the sky. At any moment, enemy bombers would be overhead.

Henry contemplated the problem without the distraction of Cameron who had stepped out to for a toilet break. He took a new packet of Woodbines from the bench and inhaled the exhilarating flavour. He removed the crisp silver paper, opened the top and from the packet, slid out a perfect white cylinder of fresh tobacco. Across the room, the telephone was jangling on Cameron's desk, the direct line to R-Block. Henry placed the cigarette in his mouth, took a book of Vestas and tore a cardboard match from its spine. He brought his thumb down along the sandpaper strip, igniting the match, leaving his fingertip black, over the hardened callous grown from so many such little burns. Slowly raising the match, he lit the cigarette. There was a tiny flame as the tobacco and paper burned, leaving a red glowing end that shone in the poor light. Henry sucked on the Woodbine and relaxed with the realisation that this problem also presented an opportunity. He bent and checked that the earth wand was still disconnected, useless. His shoulders dropped, and he felt the warmth radiate from his lungs, around his chest, encircling his whole body. As his mind cleared; he opened the steel cabinet to display the transmitter's entrails, its condensers, transformers, rectifiers and pre-amplifiers. But he knew their operation was not the problem. The PA Valve appeared to be the problem. Was it a connection, or was it one of the other valves? Possibly one valve that, due to a short circuit, sucked the current from the others, rendering the transmitter useless. Then the solution became clear.

Henry felt the burn as the embers of the cigarette approached his lips. He narrowed his eyes, squinting against the nip of the smoke. He lit another Vesta, and by its light, he saw something not quite right – the heaters were dead. He removed the cigarette from his mouth and spat away a piece of tobacco. Behind him Sergeant Cameron flew in. Holding up his trousers with one hand, he slammed the blast door, the telephone bells still ringing, the klaxon wailing outside.

"What the heck! A raid! The transmitter is down!"

Henry raised his voice.

"The PA is goosed. It's the heaters, sir."

Cameron ran straight to the transmitter cabinet, still buttoning his fly.

"Sir, the earth wand."

The earth wand lay at the side of the cabinet, its disconnected wire unseen by Cameron.

"Sir, I've not earthed the hots. They're still live."

Henry smiled, his heart pounding, the telephone still jangling on the desk. Pushing Henry out of the way, Cameron grabbed the useless earth wand, reached inside the cabinet and and used it to touch the hotspots. Instinctively, he put his palm on the glass of a hot valve. At the shock of the burn, he placed his other hand on the anode terminal — still charged at twelve thousand volts. The hotspots had not been made safe by the earth wand. In that instant, Cameron looked at Henry, mouthing the word 'Christ!' There was a bang, accompanied by a plume of smoke. The officer shuddered and fell to the floor, hanging by his hand which remained attached, the skin fused to the high voltage point. As his body slowly slid to the floor, there was a smell of cooked meat; his body twitching, smoke puffing out of his fingertips, out of the sockets of his eyes.

Harbour Street Backpacker's Hostel, Kirkwall
Friday 24th December 2010

There was a sharp knock. Jerzy closed his computer reached across the tiny room and opened the door.

"Mister Przybylski, I am Oleg Komolovsky."

Behind Komolovsky stood Ruslan and Ludmilla, staring straight ahead.

"I know who you are. What do you want with me?"

"You are Jerzy, yes?"

Komolovsky held out his hand. Jerzy ignored it, sneaking the laptop under a pillow.

"May I come in?"

"No. We can go outside."

"It is snowing again, but perhaps this makes you feel at home, no?"

Jerzy took his coat and closed the door behind him as they walked out into Harbour Street where a pair of black SUVs were parked. The snow stung their faces. The weary bodyguards exchanged uncomplaining glances.

"What do you want with me?"

"Let us talk in my car."

"I do not like this. I know you... you Russians."

"Mr Przybylski. I wish you no harm. There is someone who would like to meet with you."

Ludmilla opened the door of one of the vehicles. Komolovsky gestured towards the person inside.

"This is my colleague, Mister Rust?"

"Ah, Jerzy, isn't it? I am pleased to meet you at last. Please come in to the warm."

Jerzy nodded, carefully stepping into the vehicle, looking around him. He kept one foot out in the snow. Komolovsky smiled.

"Mister Przybylski, do you not think, if we were going to kidnap you, we would have been a little more, how shall I say, efficient? Please come into the car."

Rust laughed as Komolovsky sat in the front seat. Jerzy smiled a nervous smile and kicked the snow from his shoes.

"Ok, but I do not like this."

He closed the door, keeping a grip on the handle. Rust shivered.

"Thanks, keep the warm in. You don't mind if I call you Jerzy, do you?"

Jerzy looked Rust up and down, his tracksuit, his roseate cheeks, then Komolovsky, with his tan, his expensive suit, polished shoes.

"Mister Rust, you are not Russian?"

"Orkney born and bred."

"Why do you associate with this man, this Russian?"

"Let us say we have common interests for the good of these islands. We are businessmen."

"What do you want with me? I return to Krakow as soon as I can."

"As soon as the police release you."

Jerzy bristled.

"I am, how do they say here, I am helping them in their enquiries."

"I think you were involved with the death of the old man out at Lopness."

"I know nothing of this man."

His name was Henry Long.

Jerzy stiffened.

Rust shifted in his seat, facing Jerzy.

"I met him, you see, on the ferry to Hoy just two weeks ago; an old, troubled man. He mentioned your name."

"Why would I want to have anything to do with such a man?"

"You do know him, you see. You wanted to help him too. He told me that on the ferry."

"What? What things did he tell you?"

"Don't worry, Jerzy, we won't tell the police, will we Oleg?"

"Do not worry," Komolovsky mumbled from the front seat. Rust continued:

"I... how would you put it; I find your involvement with someone like Henry Long appealing."

"Why would you be interested in such a thing? Are you not businessman?"

Rust smiled. "I like to think of myself as something of a philosopher. I find the idea of death fascinating. I also want to help people, perhaps people who might wish to be not on this earth. So, you see, I would like to know more of your techniques."

Jerzy twitched, looking around the car. Outside, the two bodyguards sat in the other SUV. The snow on the windows created a film that slowly obscured the view. "The ether, it is painless." He breathed in deeply, tasting the air in the car, the smell of the upholstery, the deodorant, the aftershave from the two men. "He was dead when I saw him. I just made him comfortable and said a few words over his body. He was troubled man."

"A sinner?"

"We are all sinners."

"What else did you do, Jerzy?"

"Nothing."

"That is not true."

"I said prayers for his soul... I left him something for his journey."

Oleg turned around, placing his arm on the headrest.

"You gave him bread and salt."

Jerzy Przybylski looked out to the snow. Rust touched his arm.

"For the journey."

Jerzy nodded.

"Interesting."

"That is all. I did it to take away his sins. I did not kill him."

"We understand, Jerzy. You did a good thing."

Jerzy wiped away a tear.

"Now I want to go home."

Oleg handed a small hip flask back to Jerzy.

"Vodka?"

Jerzy nodded, gulped back the spirit and shivered.

Lambholm Airstrip, Holm
Friday 24th December 2010

Christine drove past the Italian Chapel, over the rise, approaching Churchill Barrier Number two. Komolovsky was talking on a mobile phone while his bodyguards scanned the road, up and down as traffic passed. He waved as Christine pulled in, slipping his phone into his pocket. He opened the door of her Mazda, and kissed her cheek, holding her hand as she stepped out of the car. She blushed, looked away, and smiled.

"Privyet, Christine."

"Hello, Oleg. I came. I'm not sure I should have, but I did."

"You are here now; that is all that matters. Come this way."

Christine eyed the man and woman in their dark suits.

"Let me introduce my friends, Ruslan and Ludmilla."

Christine laughed. "That's what you call them?"

"That is what I call them."

Komolovsky led Christine up a short slope to a cleared area with an orange windsock and a hangar. Parked inside was a gleaming white light aircraft with a bubble canopy. Ruslan and Ludmilla pushed the microlight out into the open.

"You're joking, Oleg. We're going flying?"

"It is a beautiful day, is it not?"

Komolovsky walked around the aircraft, examining the flight controls, moving them back and forward. He checked various bolts and parts for movement. On the other side of the grass strip, Christine recognised John Flear, standing by a tractor, near a mound of snow. He raised his hand in recognition. Christine waved back discreetly.

"I must perform these checks before we fly. I must confirm that it is safe before we take off."

"Of course."

"This is the Pitot tube. The altimeter detects the air pressure in this tube. It must be clear always, especially when it is cold. If it ices up this would be a problem."

Oleg waved away Ruslan and Ludmilla, opened the canopy and gestured for Christine to climb in. In the tiny cockpit, they were close, their shoulders touching. Christine giggled nervously.

"I've never done anything like this before."

"Are you nervous, Christine?"

"A little, maybe."

Komolovsky carried on with the pre-flight checks, setting the trim to neutral, flaps, lights, fuel. He leaned over, checked Christine's harness and squeezed her hand. Oleg started the engine and the little aircraft shuddered into life. Christine placed a headset over her ears, and immediately the engine noise disappeared; all she could hear was Oleg's breathing. He taxied the aircraft to face the wind and checked the control surfaces once again, examining the instruments, referring to the laminated checklist by his knee. He reached over Christine so that their bodies came into contact; he pulled on the door handle.

"We don't want you to fall out."

Christine nodded.

"Can you hear me, Christine? You have to speak to check the comms."

"Sorry. Yes, I can hear you, Over."

Komolovsky smiled.

"Is that Ok?"

"Yes, that is all good. Christine."

The airstrip had been cleared of snow and markers delineated the boundaries of the grass landing strip, still covered in a film of white. As the little aircraft taxied out to the holding point, the crackling voice of the controller at Kirkwall passed on weather and flight information. Oleg started the roll, bumping over the icy grass surface. As the end of the runway approached faster and faster, Christine held her breath; just when there was only the sea ahead, the aircraft lifted off, heading east before banking right and north. On the ground, Christine saw John Flear, waving, behind him, the Italian Chapel, its red highlights sharp against the snow.

They flew low over Holm. Past the Churchill Barrier Number One, with the rusted hulks of the blockships visible, their full size clear below the water, Oleg spoke with the control tower at Kirkwall airport, his breathing audible between each transmission.

"I will be crossing the approach path into the airport, so I have to check it is clear to do so."

Christine nodded, looking all around. To their left was the expanse of Scapa Flow, the flame at Flotta licking the sky; ahead of them, the Scapa distillery, its massive black on white logo on the bond just to the left of the beach. Below them to the right was the pagoda roof of Highland Park and the road into Kirkwall; St Magnus' spire governing everything. It was as if the spire was now their sole point of reference, their datum in the whole turning world. They pointed to it and to other landmarks, Christine nodding eagerly, scanning the islands below, trying not to miss anything. Oleg said something lost in the static, pointing out to the north and west, at a shape on the edge of the Bay of Kirkwall. "Pardon?" said Christine.

"I said, there is my 'Vorona'."

Komolovsky veered left over the harbour, out to his ship, circling it.

"I must tell you that my missile will be trained on us, waiting for us to do anything threatening."

"What? Oleg. My God, a guided missile, you're not serious."
Komolovsky laughed.

"We are safe, Christine. The guided missile, it is disabled for the moment, but the radar, it is active."

"Maybe we shouldn't fly too close."

Christine watched the strange form of the 'Vorona' meld and move, shifting from one shape to the next as they flew around it, its black mass dominating the empty space of water, sharply contrasting with the snow-covered landscape beyond.

"I can't make out the shape. It doesn't look like a boat. It looks like a crow from a distance."

"Vorona."

"Yes, but it looks different depending on which angle you look at it. I really can't tell what it is. Is that what they call the stealth technology?"

"Perhaps. I think it is more the imagination of my friend, Phillippe in Paris. He designed 'Vorona'. He is a very insightful man."

They flew over Shapinsay, towards Sanday; below them the Start Point Lighthouse, bright against the snow, a vivid column of white and black. Here, at two thousand feet, Christine's worries evaporated in the free air. They flew all the way to North Ronaldsay. She saw the dots of the sheep moving on the snow-flecked seaweed that bordered the beach. All around the islands, the cold grey of the sea blended into the persistent white that covered everything.

"I've never seen so much snow on Orkney. There is no green, anywhere."

"The green will return in spring. I see this in Russia every year. It makes you appreciate more the colour of life, its force, its energy. You should see Russia in the spring. Ah, Christine; *Sibir', krasivaya Sibir'*, Such a beautiful land. It is my soul. It can be yours too, Christine. *Poydem so mnoy v Rossiyu, Kristina; pozhaluysta?*"

Christine was comfortable in the small cockpit, the sound of Oleg's breathing, the feeling the heat on her feet, and the warmth of Oleg's shoulder.

"I don't know Oleg; I just don't know."

Komolovsky banked the plane. To her left, Christine saw only the sea, to her right, the sky. Oleg kept the aircraft in this configuration for what seemed a long time, until it was flying level, then flew south once more.

"Would you like to fly the aeroplane?"

"I couldn't. I've never done it before."

"It is not difficult. You take controls, like this..."

Komolovsky put Christine's hands onto the control column, one hand over hers.

"There. You have control."

"So it would seem."

Oleg let go.

"Just keep it in a straight line. Shall we fly over your home in Finstown?"

Christine shuddered; the aircraft lurched in the clear air.

"Whoa, let me take control."

Komolovsky settled the plane on a smooth course again.

"Would you?"

Christine thought of her husband, messing about in his study. For a moment, she worried if he was Ok.

"Yes, that would be nice."

* * *

Clett heard the buzzing of a light aircraft. Turning his chair from the desk, he looked out the window, observing the small plane circling overhead. He went out into the garden and approached the rowan tree, touching its three intertwined trunks, examining the boughs. While the tree still had a handful of bright red berries, one bough was bare. He stretched up, took a branch and broke it. It crumbled, dry, lifeless in his hand.

nitroglycerin

T-Block, RAF Whale Head
Saturday 12th December 1942

Henry reconnected the earth wand and grounded the hotspots. He dragged Jack Cameron's blackened body out of sight, behind the cabinet, holding his breath against the stench of cooked flesh that filled his nostrils.

The air-raid siren continued its whine; Henry couldn't think in the cacophony. His focus was now to get the transmitter working. He needed a cigarette and his hands shook. As he peered once more inside the transmitter cabinet, the telephone jangled, rattling on its hook. Henry wiped Cameron's charred skin from his palms and lifted the receiver.

"Yes, the transmitter is down."

"How long before it is restored?" snapped the person on the other end of the line.

"How long before it is restored?" Henry repeated the question and stared at the lifeless steel cabinet.

"I don't know."

"What do you mean, you don't know?" Have you no understanding of how important this is. Let me speak to the commanding technical officer."

The smoke rose from Cameron's body.

"He's in the khazi. I'll get him to telephone you."

* * *

Without RDF, Charlotte examined her plotting notes. Right up until the failure of the signal, she was clear the bombers were following the same track as the last raid. She repeated her calculations, paused for a second, and engaged the 'press to talk' switch.

"Whale Head unserviceable. Target tracks of hostiles following same track as previous raids. Suspect enemy not targeting Scapa, but estimate targeting Whale Head; repeat, estimate enemy raid on Whale Head."

* * *

Henry opened the cabinet to examine the high voltage components. There was no sign of arcing. Studying the circuit drawings, it was clear that the problem was not the final power circuits; it still appeared to be the heaters.

Behind him, the door opened, and the station commander rushed in, he sniffed and grimaced. Henry stood between him and Cameron's body behind the transmitter.

"Why aren't you answering your phone? Why are you not advising operations about a return of service?"

Henry remained silent, staring at the Station Officer, eyes blazing, cheeks crimson with fury.

The Station Officer barked:

"What is the problem, man?"

"I'm not sure sir, it could be a faulty heater."

"In God's name, change it!"

"But sir it appears to be undamaged. There's no sign of damage to the filaments."

"Damn you, what is it then?"

"Sir, I'm not sure, the rectifier might be the problem."

"Well, for God's sake change it... and what is that burning smell? It's disgusting."

"A rat found its way into the transmitter cabinet, sir."

Outside the klaxon continued its distracting rise and fall, stopping Henry from thinking straight. Somewhere in the sky above were an unknown number of German bombers, their sole task: the obliteration of Whale Head.

"The rectifier is a new component, replaced last week. Sir, I need to think."

"Think! Don't think! Just do it, boy."

Henry shook; unable to respond, unable to analyse the situation under the barking questions of the Station Officer and the overwhelming noise from the air-raid siren. He put his hands over his ears to concentrate.

"Have you no idea, boy? This base, and possibly the British fleet, is at risk, and you can't make up your damned mind."

"Sir, it might be the heater transformer. Look, there's oil leaking from the case."

"What are you waiting for, man! In God's name change it. How long will it take? I expect the service to be restored in ten minutes or I will have you on a court martial – if we live long enough."

The Station Officer looked around the transmitter room.

"Where is your senior officer, anyway?"

As Henry stuttered a response, a clerk entered, giving the Station Officer a signal. As he read it, the blood drained from his face.

"A Squadron of German bombers has been detected possibly now within forty miles, on a direct track here, to this station. My God! Get this equipment working."

He turned and ran back to the receiver block.

To the south, at Scapa Flow, carbon elements cracked and sparked in the searchlights that swung through the sky, illuminating the barrage balloons, their beams criss-crossing each other. Twenty-five miles to the east, five Heinkel bombers flew in a skein towards their target. In the night sky, to their left, the crews could see the lights of Scapa Flow, protected by hundreds of barrage balloons, surrounded by the anti-aircraft guns, too risky a target for their mission. They continued north, in the direction of Whale Head.

In T-Block, Henry lit another cigarette and held a match to see in to the top of the heater transformer. There was something wrong with the connector. Screwing his eyes, he took a long draw on the cigarette, presented a spanner to a loose connector, and made it fast. He sucked the smoke, his lips burning. In one motion, he lit another cigarette from the remains of the old one, extinguishing the cinders between his fingers, not minding the pain, dropping the fag end on to a little pile of douts[6]. Having checked the position of the connector, he closed the doors, switched on the transmitter and waited for the high voltages to establish. Within a few long minutes the cabinet became warm, pulsing, reflecting its aurora

---

[6] Dout – fag-end, remains of a cigarette.

around the room, illuminating the partly incinerated body of Sergeant Sandy Cameron.

In the sky above, the Heinkels were closing. Charlotte watched as the CRT came to life, the dancing green phosphor now swamping the screen.

With the transmitter functioning, Henry went out into the darkening sky and the roar of the Heinkels. Up past his exhaled smoke, into the canopy above, he saw the bomb, falling directly over his head, tumbling, rotating, until it settled into its downwards trajectory. He ran from T-Block along the concrete path, feeling the icy drizzle on his face, and the taste of iron in his throat as he gasped. Henry was in mid-stride when the bomb exploded, the shock wave carrying him through the air.

The Clett Home, Finstown
Friday 24th December 2010

Magnus and Sandy Clett levered a joint of ham out of the oven, accompanied by a cloud of spicy steam. In the lounge, there was the chatter of Roland and Christine, and Magnus' fiancée Jane, sitting around their Christmas Tree. Outside, the dark night was lit with light snow blown into soft drifts.

"Have you set a date for the wedding?"

"We're going for June 7th. Think we might be able to get the cathedral."

"Oh, that would be just lovely," said Christine.

There was a clatter from the kitchen.

"Food's ready."

They sat at the table and clinked glasses.

"It's so nice we're all together. So glad you boys got the ferry, and with Jane too. This is so special. I wish we could do this more."

Magnus filled his mother's glass.

"Do you know, Mum, in quantum physics, they say it's possible for two particles at opposite ends of the cosmos to affect each other. In fact, they are exactly dependent on each other and can't exist independently. When one spins, so does the other, when one changes its energy level, so does the other. I reckon that this is like our family. We spin in the same direction no matter how far apart we are."

"At other ends of the cosmos? That's nice."

"They call it 'entanglement'."

Sandy raised his glass.

"Here's to our entanglements."

They clinked their glasses again.

"Well, I think it's nonsense, Magnus. Nice metaphor, but that's all."

"It's quantum physics, Dad."

Christine sipped her wine.

"Well, Roland, I think it is a lovely idea. A quantum family."

Sandy looked at his father.

"And the Ba' tomorrow, Dad! Are you nervous?"

"Me?" Clett smiled. "After the last few weeks, it'll be a release for all that tension."

Christine went to the window, moving the curtain, and looked out over the Bay of Firth, east to where the 'Vorona' was moored in Kirkwall Bay, its black form changing shape in the night, unseen against the dark sky beyond the veil of snow. Under her breath, she mouthed: "Entanglement."

Broad Street, Kirkwall
Saturday 25th December 2010
Fifteen minutes before the start of the Christmas Day Ba'

In front of St Magnus' Cathedral, three hundred players waited for the game of the Ba'. They were wrapped in layers of t-shirts and sweaters, trousers tucked inside thick socks; some had duct-tape wrapped around their laces. Uppies and Doonies shook hands, in anticipation of the moments to come, of joy and anger and not knowing. Some nervously kicked the snow from their shoes. Around and among them were friends and spectators, keeping warm with flasks of tea or a dram.

In the good-natured crowd, in the mix of gallus boys with their thumbs in their belt buckles, the older men casting an eye on the newcomers, Magnus and Sandy Clett smiled at their father as they waited for the cathedral clock to strike one. The frosty air was still, packed snow and ice lay underfoot. There was murmuring from the crowd and the odd cough, amplified and reflected between the cathedral and the Town Hall, the exhaled air from the men forming a fog of vapour over their heads.

The noise of the pack was like a low rumble, a slow rise in tension felt by everyone. As the players compressed in anticipation, Clett could smell the sweat from the men beside him. He looked around the two or three faces visible to him in the crush, and at Sandy who was grinning. They had lost sight of Magnus. It was going to be impossible to keep together. In the moments leading up to the start of the game, the crowd of bodies pushed and surged. Clett looked up to the cathedral clock. The minute hand lurched to one o'clock, and, as the bell struck, the Ba' was flung far into the outstretched arms of the assembled Uppies and Doonies. A roar went up from the players and the spectators. The Ba' immediately disappeared into the body of men as it moved back towards the Town Hall and quickly stabilised into an immovable mass, with satellite players quickly getting into position at the periphery, trying to rotate the scrum, to turn it away from the support of the Town Hall Wall; to fragment it and its interlocked mass. At the edge of the pack, players were losing their grip on the ice.

The scrum heaved, as if it were one entity, breathing in and out, the bodies in the middle crushed, unable to affect the direction of movement, lost to the sway and swoon of the mass of men.

Suddenly the scrum broke up, and they all accelerated, slipping and sliding on the ice and snow, in the direction of the harbour.

"Aye. It'll be a quick game this year."

"Nae chance."

"Like 'eighty-five. I'm telling ye. Four, mibbe five minutes noo."

The game of the Ba' was known to last many hours, or a few minutes. Could it be over so soon? For no reason, the scrum had broken into a swarm of men running along Broad Street. Clett ran with the crowd, looking for clues as to who held the Ba'. As always, most of the players could only guess as to its location: hidden in plain view, on a windowsill with everyone running past, left in a house, or tucked under a sweatshirt. In the cycles of expectation and confusion could be heard occasional shouts of "Uppies hae the Ba'" or "Ba' here," but experienced players would be sceptical. Sometimes they used code words, but these quickly became unusable either through the excitement of the players, or the other side spotting a new phrase in the mix.

Over at the Peedie Sea, boys who were placed to look out for the weather were texting.

"Beuys, it's blawin' fea the west," and "Naethin guid."

The weather updates from the messages gave a clear signal that was by now apparent to the players. A whiteout was imminent.

With the change in the weather, some spectators turned back to the pubs, and some responded to invitations to have a meal or a dram at a friend's house. But most just kept on going, pushing on in near zero visibility. The players now could not tell the top of the ball from the bottom, but every so often the Ba' came out of the blizzard.

Clett could see Sandy through the dense cloud of human steam above the clutch of men crushing each other, pushing and grunting, oblivious of the thick snow surrounding them, sometimes just aware of the odd snowflake fluttering past their head. This part of the game was one of those periods of quiet effort. No ground was lost or gained, and it was an opportunity for some to rest while keeping the momentum going. They all knew that this stasis could not last. At some point, it might be in a moment or in an hour's time, unexpectedly, someone would get a touch, or a smuggle would be attempted, or a dummy sold and the scrum would dissolve, players sprinting away until faced with a blocked lane or a cul-de-sac or, if the other side communicated well enough, another impenetrable body of men that might block play.

The pack had now re-amalgamated and stalled at the Big Tree in Albert Street. This was a well-known point where, because of the supports of the tree and the barricaded shop windows, the scrum could remain solid and immobile. Today this was exactly what happened. The men crept unwittingly, turning and slipping and grunting with the pack, Uppies and Doonies limbs locked so close that one man would breathe in the exhaled air of the man next to him. Together, unwillingly, but engaging with this piece of animal poetry where a kind of magic, an unidentifiable force, drove them on; individuals attempting to assert their will against a solid mass of heaving human inertia.

There was a mist of vapour over the good-humoured pack; it throbbed, the players shouting to each other. Clett saw the face of Ronnie Rust next to him, and then he disappeared. The sight of Rust brought him up short. He searched around for him in the the mass of Uppies and Doonies, but he was lost in the mass of players.

As it happened, not five feet away, Rust had achieved a place right in the middle of the pack, pushing to make a space for John McPherson who had the Ba'. He spoke in his ear.

"It's all good, John. We need to get you to the outside so ye can try a smuggle. I'll mak' a peedie wee diversion."

An arm's length away, out of sight, Clett gestured to John Turnbull, one of the outer Uppie players. He had lost sight of Sandy and Magnus, and was pushing against the scrum, up towards Bridge Street.

As he pushed, the men were stuck together like dovetailed joints, unable to move. Clett relaxed, allowing the pressure of the players around him to keep him upright, when out of nowhere he felt a blow to his nose which exploded in a splash of blood. In his daze, he saw Ronnie Rust's malicious grin. There was another blow and he felt himself lose consciousness, slipping slowly to the ground.

Clett tried to turn over, to get on his feet. He saw the blood dribble on to the ice and looked around for someone injured before realising the blood was his. All he could see were the feet of the players around him, clad in coloured trainers, socks and laces sealed with duct-tape. He tried to protect himself by crouching down.

"Man down. For fuck's sake, make a space. Man down! C'mon guys."

Slowly, the pressure in the pack eased as a space was made. Clett felt the scrum ease around him. As he was helped to his feet, he saw the front of his jumper covered in blood.

"Make way, make way there."

In his confusion, in the cotton wool sound of the scrum on the snow, Clett was sure he heard the voice of Ronnie Rust. Did Rust hit him? How could he be sure? The pack parted to make way for Clett, staggering and dazed, out into the open. Heavy snow continued to fall. Clett turned to the man supporting him and saw Ronnie Rust's face, their breath condensing, combining in the freezing air.

"You…"

"You're welcome, Inspector. Hae a good Ba'!"

Rust turned back, pushing his way back into the pack. Bewildered, Clett looked around him as he sat down on the kerb at the Royal Bank corner.

"Inspector. Fuck me! Sorry, but whit a mess is your fizz."

Clett looked up dejectedly into the faces of Irene and Sanja, and he tried a smile.

"Jeez, let's get this blood aff yur face." Clett watched in amazement as Sanja and Irene took from their handbags the components of a full first aid kit. They tidied him, dabbing and prodding, applying cotton buds and a few steri-strips.

"This is some game you huv here, Inspector. Pure brilliant. Were you in that scrum?"

Clett nodded.

"Christ, there must be three hundred men in that pack. I'd like to see the health and safety analysis for this."

"Don't even think about it," grunted Clett.

Without warning, the pack broke again, and all the players split, most running down West Castle Street, some in the opposite direction, some running down Albert Street. Clett, Sanja and Irene could hear the confusion in the calls of the players:

"What happened?"

"I heard the Ba's back at Victoria Street."

"Cannae see it ma'sel'. I heard there was a Doonie beuy smuggle-and-run tae the ither end o' Albert Street."

Sanja caught Irene's eye: "Naeb'dy kens onything."

"Aye, looks kinda confusin'. Is this normal Inspector? Are there nae rules?"

"No rules, Sanja."

"How can they even tell who is in their team wi' so many players?"

"Aye, it's confusing right enough."

Irene gave Clett a bottle of water. As the runners thinned out, Clett saw Jerzy Przybylski across the street. Sanja held a cotton wool ball to Clett's right nostril.

"Inspector, please just keep your head up. It will let the blood clot."

Irene opened a bag and cleaned the blood from Clett's face with a wipe. Jerzy approached the trio at the kerb. "I believe you were hurt in the game, and your friends carried you out."

Jerzy coughed and turned away, busying himself with his phone, taking photographs of the scrum, disappearing around the corner into at the other end of Albert Street; the snow created an almost monochrome image, as if from an old television picture, the distant image fading to grey. Clett slouched on the kerb and shook his head.

"Chin up, Inspector," said Sanja.

With the persistent snow, the air was stilled, the calls of the crowd a few streets away, now lost, muffled by the new fall.

"Dad, what happened?"

"Magnus. You ok?"

"Yeah, Dad. This is bloody great, but what about you? Is your nose broken?"

"I'm not sure. I don't think so."

"Naw," said Irene. "He'll be jist fine."

"I touched the Ba' Da."

"When?"

"Just a few minutes ago. John Turnbull was trying a smuggle."

"Have you seen Magnus?"

"Not since the start."

Around them, players walked up and down, climbing garden walls, standing around, looking for the Ba'. A street away could be heard the intermittent baying of car alarms. Out of the wandering players and spectators, Christine approached with Jane, smiling. She opened a thermos flask and silently poured him some tea. As Clett slowly gained his senses, he looked at Christine and grinned.

"It's dot as bad as it looks. I don' t'ink my dose is broken."

"Nae chance," said Irene. "Ah'm tellin' ye, ye'll be fine, Inspector."

"Roland, I despair."

Clett held on to Christine's hand on his shoulder. Magnus was looking down the street after the split scrum, the receding dull roar softly reflected between the buildings.

"Well, Jane, are you enjoying your first Ba'?"

"Very much, Magnus. It is exciting and it is loco, is it not?"

"Aye, Jane. Loco. I'll buy that. How's your nose, Dad?"

"It's fine. Get back in the game, Magnus."

"Sure you'll be ok?"

"Aye, off you go."

"The scrum is all over the place, and nobody knows where the Ba' is."

Clett shrugged his shoulders: "Don't ask me."

Magnus kissed Jane and grinned as he turned and raced back across the ice, finding the larger pack locked into the library railings, and he slid, shoving into the steaming mass of panting shouting men.

"And again; push!"

Sanja and Irene helped Clett to his feet, and, along with Christine, walked back down West Castle Street, past Radio Orkney towards the library and the scrum, now attracting all the wandering players like a magnet. Jerzy caught up with them. He coughed.

"Inspector. Have you recovered?"

"I think so, Jerzy. Are you enjoying the game?"

"It is… what is that word? It is visceral."

Clett nodded. "That is indeed the word, Jerzy."

"Yes, visceral. It has a contained, perhaps... affectionate, yes, an affectionate violence."

The group stood in front of the pack, throbbing and heaving, breathing as a single entity, between the ice and snow, and the cloud of vapour that floated in the air above them. Jerzy paused. He was tired and had not slept.

"Inspector. I would like to go home to Krakow. Am I still a suspect?"

A tired voice from the scrum called: "Ba' here, Ba' here. Tae the Uppies."

Clett faced Jerzy. "I have a fair idea of what happened, Jerzy."

"You do? Did you speak with the Russian, and with Mister Rust?"

At the mention of Rust's name, Clett looked down at his feet.

"Not about you, Jerzy. My concerns are of different matters. No Jerzy, you can go home."

"Thank you, Inspector. I need to go back to Krakow."

"Do that, Jerzy, but be careful. I think you care too much. Go back to your mathematics."

"Inspector, I cannot say what is ahead of me now. I am not in control of my fate. I am like those confused players who don't know who has the ball."

"The Ba', Jerzy, the Ba'."

"The Ba', Inspector."

Jerzy and Clett shook hands and parted. The pack seemed to be gaining energy once again. Without warning, Christine handed the thermos flask to Clett, kissed him on the mouth, smiled, and turned towards the scrum. Followed by Sanja and Irene and Jane, she walked over and started pushing with some other women, laughing and shouting. They could see the group begin to rotate and there was some agitation returning. Clett couldn't believe what he was seeing.

"Christine..."

Someone shouted:

"That's no very lady-like."

As Clett watched, Christine disappeared around the other side of the heaving mass. He held a bloody hanky and the thermos and went around to find her.

Clett felt a hand on his back. It was Archie Drever.

"I heard you were going in for the Ba', but I wouldn't have

believed it until I saw it. What have you done to yourself, Roland?"

"It was Rust..."

"What?"

"In the scrum, he hit me."

"How can you be sure? It looked to me as if he got you out of trouble."

"No, well, I don't know, but I'm sure he hit me. Have you seen Christine? She went into the scrum."

"What?"

Through the pack, and out of the corner of his eye, he glimpsed Christine in Tankerness Lane, talking to someone he couldn't see. Was it Komolovsky? Clett pushed his way through and got to the spot, but she had disappeared.

There was a shout and the mass of players quickly fragmented once more with everyone running towards the Basin. A few minutes later, the pack had re-amalgamated all along the Harbour Street railing. Clett found Magnus and Sandy and stood with them, looking down into the freezing water of the Basin.

"The Ba's gone doon!"

In the gloom, the odd flurry of snow blew through the streetlights, but in the cold shallow water of the Basin, ten Doonie men were engaged in an unknown argument, a secret series of claims and offers and cajoles, their voices lost in the sounds of the dull shouts from the remaining players and supporters. What commentators were calling a 'negotiation' was taking place among the Doonies in the water, a sequence of embraces, and slaps on the back, with shouts and hidden words and the odd push and shove. As the Ba' was held aloft and hurled once more into the icy harbour, followed by players jumping into the freezing water, the crowd shouted and pushed, and at the rear still could not be sure that the game was approaching its conclusion.

Then: "Doonie's Ba'!"

Above the splashing water and shouting, Clett heard: "Mister Rust's Ba'."

Clett peered down into the Basin and saw Rust holding the Ba', up to his waist in the icy water. In amazement, he watched as Rust gave the Ba' to the man next to him, clapping him on the shoulder. He heard Rust's voice: "John McPherson's Ba'! John McPherson's Ba'!"

"Mister Rust has given the Ba' tae another Doonie."

All the players in the Basin clapped and congratulated Ronnie

Rust, nodding and smiling as he held aloft a grinning John McPherson. A roar went up in the crowd as the new winner was raised on to the shoulders of his team-mates. Above them, a cloud of vapour.

CHAPTER EIGHTEEN

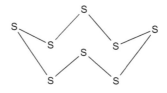

brimstone

RAF Whale Head
Saturday 12th December 1942

Henry heard only a high-pitched whistle. He lay on the heather for a long time, considering if he was dreaming or awake. He looked around him; two of the masts supporting the transmitter array had been hit and were lying bent in the sky, sagging, their guys and wires hanging from them like lost sheets on a sad ship.

Beyond the sound in his head, Henry heard a distant klaxon. He covered his ears, but it made the whistling louder. Strangely, through all the chaos and noise, there were the sounds of pigeons in the nearby doocot, fluffing and cooing, rearranging their nests in their stone structure, clear and upright in the debris and dust. A dog padded up and licked Henry's face. He shoo'ed him away and peered through the smoke. T-Block and R-Block were in ruins; several smaller fires were dotted around the site. He had been half-way between the two concrete bunkers when bombs hit both sites.

The dog whimpered, looking hopefully at Henry. At R-Block, the blast door was buckled and jammed closed. Henry climbed the scorched grass slope and looked down into the operations room, through the space in the open roof that had been created by the bomb. The whole area was thick with grey dust, a few licks of flame coming from the bent remains of the equipment. The scene was monochrome and silent, intermittently illuminated by little electrical flashes. He climbed down to the floor of the operation room and saw lumps in the grey. He went to one of the shapes and bent down. In the grim murk, he saw the outline of a human form, the charred remains of a woman lying on her face. Henry knew from her outline, even in death, that special curve of her hips.

Olfsquoy Estate, Kirkwall
Sunday 26th December 2010

Ronnie Rust's phone buzzed: Janie Shearer's name on the screen.

"Hello Janie. Have you had a nice Christmas?"

"Aye, Mister Rust, lovely, just me and my wee girl, Jessie."

"Aye, you've got a wee charmer there. I hope Santa was good to her?"

"That he was, Mister Rust. Thanks for asking, I am actually calling to congratulate you on your performance at The Ba'. It was a fine thing you did."

"It was the right thing to do, Janie."

"Well, it has caught the attention of many people. Social media is going mad about it. Your name is getting more visibility than the winner. All this can only be good for you."

"It is what it is, Janie. One step at a time. The council elections will be next."

"Well, that looks like a done deal, Mister Rust, but have you thought about what comes after that?"

"Funny you should ask that, Janie. They say the weather in Edinburgh is softer than up here. Who knows?"

* * *

Adair Crawford MD FRS
Royal Military Academy
Woolwich
Dec 12th 1789

Sir,
I write to you concerning your paper to the
Royal Society on Nov 10th, 'On the Medicinal
Qualities of Muriated Barytes'. You refer to
your investigations into the qualities of your
new earth, Strontianite, and you describe a
method of distinguishing your new earth
from Barium. The red flame of the ore of
Strontium distinguishing it from Barium. I
congratulate you on the discovery of your
new earth. May it find a future in our
changing world, and may its discovery bring
you happiness.

Sir, I write to you as a humble philosopher,
interested in our fashionable human search
for new names for all things, of our
endeavour to place our ideas in juxtaposition
to one another, each separate and connected.
I am happy that you have named this new
earth as Strontianite. Like the good Mister
Arrhenius in Stockholm who has so
celebrated the little place of Ytterby, you
have celebrated such little places by the
dignity of a new name in Natural Philosophy.

Further, while sharing your yearning with
the need to separate out all that is our world,
to list each new element, I am concerned
about the future of such an approach. In
identifying new substances, new compounds,
are we not entering upon a quest that will
never end? Who is to know what end is there
for this exercise? Is there a limit on the

*substances in the universe? Even if the
substances in the world are finite, we
inevitably find our selves questioning
constituent parts in what we think now of as
indivisible elements. Is this the task of
Sisyphus that will engage Natural
Philosophers for eternity?*

*I suggest that a different narration may fit.
That is to consider all that is around us as
contiguous. That we live in a soup of
existence, from which we men are
indistinguishable. We are not thus
individuals, but are part of a connected
whole, bound to each other in an ether, a
field of influence that enmeshes us together,
the action of each affecting that of the other.
Everything we do affects another. This ether
permeates all, us and each other. Thus, in its
binding way, it makes our actions have direct
effects on others, rippling out into time, the
consequences unknown to us, the actors.*

Yr. Most Humble Servant

Arch. Clett of Canmore

The Clett Home, Finstown
Sunday 26th December 2010

Sanja and Irene rang the Clett's doorbell.

"Are you sure this is the hoose?"

"Yup. That's his auld Polo."

"So it is. Why does he drive such a wreck?"

"I don't think he cares about new things. Christine's Mazda is lovely, though."

"Know her well?"

"Met her a few times. Did ye no' see her at the Ba' yesterday?"

Clett answered the door.

"Hi Inspector. Merry Christmas. Have you recovered from your bump at The Ba'?"

"Aye, Sanja, and call me Roland. Thanks for coming. Come in and meet the family. You know Christine; this is Sandy and Magnus, and Magnus' fiancée, Jane. Jane's from Argentina."

"Really. How exciting! *Cómo estás?*"

"Estoy bien gracias y tu?"

"Muy bien!"

Jane shook hands with Sanja and Irene.

"I try to get Magnus to speak Spanish. It is a long road."

"We heard you're getting married in June."

"Yes, in the Cathedral. You'll have to come."

Outside, the light was low; the Christmas tree dominated the front room.

"More champagne, anyone?"

"Come on Dad, come on Mum, show us some of your steps."

"Do you dance, Inspector, er, Roland?"

"I have been known to."

Sandy fiddled with his phone and seconds later, sound came from the speakers. At the first chord, Clett held Christine's waist firmly. She moved her head back, keeping the tension. He kissed her, and she moved closer to him. With no space between them, every cavity, every hollow covered by their contact. They moved slowly and stepped into a single dance, slowly, gently covering each other's steps, their legs twined like swans' necks.

"Bloody hell, Mum."

"Beautiful, Christine, Beautiful!" said Jane, clapping. Sanja and Irene hooted.

"Go Inspector, er... Roland!"

Jane sang along: *"Sin recuerdos el olvido es rey..."*

Clett and Christine swung and swerved and swept past the space where the coffee table had been. Christine leant back, supported by Clett. There, they hesitated for the cadence, and he dragged her feet across their veneered oak floor. As Magnus, Sandy and Jane were talking, Clett and Christine's cheeks touched.

"Whoa, Mum, Dad, get a room!"

Clett placed his palm against the small of Christine's back and squeezed her close. Christine reached up and held his shoulder though his now-creased shirt. She was wearing the silk cream coloured blouse she had kept for good. This blouse had history. It rustled between her cardigan and her skin as they moved, their bodies echoing and responding, clinging together, swinging as one.

At the top of the phrase, they inhaled together, and the music rose to the climax. They slid, compressed together, in front of the sofa and along the wide vista of the window, the light on Stenness Loch diminishing in the evening, and the music came to a beautiful stop, with a chord from the bandoneon[7] and violin.

Here in a front room in Finstown in Orkney, in this North, Roland and Christine danced this dance, born in the heat of another continent.

---

[7] Bandoneon; accordion played in tango bands.

ether

Lopness, Sanday
Monday 13th December 2010

In the cold morning dim, Henry squinted at the shimmering computer screen. He ticked items on a list scribbled on a yellow pad. Beside him lay an old supermarket carrier bag with a flask, two tea lights and a box of matches.

He scanned Jerzy's old emails, from the supportive early days, to the more recent messages where he wouldn't stop with his religious stuff, all the 'redemption' nonsense. Henry knew his punishment persisted: the bitter unhappy life, the distant lives of his wife and children to whom he had left his legacy of unhappiness, wherever they were now.

Henry had made his plans, there was no point in waiting any more. Nothing was keeping him here. He had been given the permission. Yes, those words from a kind stranger. A stranger who had known suffering, who had reflected all Henry's pain. What was his name again, Mister something? What was his name? A man on a ferry that allowed him to end his life. No, there was nothing to be gained in reflecting or delaying. He had made his decision. His was just another life; a life that had no meaning since that day many years ago. He could still smell her perfume. If he closed his eyes, he could imagine the feel of the rough fabric of her grey blue uniform; but then he could also smell Cameron's burnt flesh. He still dreamed of him, with that voice, laughing at him, smoke coming from his empty eye sockets.

He moved the mouse using two knarled hands, placed the cursor over an icon that he had entitled 'goodbye'. He closed his eyes and clicked. The hard disc chattered softly; applications shut down as his program started to over-write all the data on the computer. He winced as the hair shirt under his cardigan irritated an old graze.

He turned from the computer screen, picked up his stick and opened the door out into the cold morning. He trudged the half mile to the ruins of T-Block, not feeling the cold on his bare feet. A few hundred yards from the ruined bunker, he threw the stick away, and painfully stumbled across the field. As he moved, the hair shirt irritated his skin, creating new abrasions. No one would see him, dressed in this foolish shroud. He staggered into the bunker, and prepared the scene, placing the items down. Ignoring the pain in his hands, he poured the ether into the plastic bag and placed it over his head. He breathed in the sharp fumes and instantly felt light-headed; his tongue became numb with the icy sensation that spread around his body as his vision disintegrated. He lay on the concrete floor between the two candles and felt the chill on his shoulders and on his back and legs.

With his last breath, he whispered:

"Charlotte…"

Notes

The title, 'Compass of Shame' was coined by the late Donald L. Nathanson, M.D. The term is widely used in developmental psychology and restorative justice.

The technically astute may notice that the two air-raids on Whale Head have aircraft tracked from a direction that would not have been possible with the Chain Home installation on Sanday. I have created a fictional increase in the scanned 'point of shoot' to accommodate my story.

It is impossible for Jerzy (ch3) to see sheep grazing on the beaches of North Ronaldsay from Sanday.

The term 'Radar' only came into use around 1943 and originated in America. In the UK, the initials 'RDF" – Radio Direction Finding' – were used prior to this.

There have been several versions of the phonetic alphabet in use. The version used by Charlotte and her colleagues was that used in Britain in 1942.

There really was an air raid on RAF Whale Head, after which the station was out of commission for eighteen months. It started operations again, but by then the focus of the war shifted to France and Africa, and the North Sea was now no longer seen as strategically crucial. Whale Head was used for research and shut down after the war. The accommodation blocks and NAAFI were sited at Langamay, some distance from Lopness.

The events of the 2010 New Year's Day Ba' as described here were not based on any actual events. It did not snow. To keep the record straight, and to recognise the achievements of those men, that game was won by Rodney Spence, a Doonie. I also say that the 1995 Christmas Day game was won by Nancie Keldie's father. In reality, it was won by Paul Miller, another Doonie.

Acknowledgements

Thanks are due to my editor, Claire Wingfield, who has been an astute observer of what has needed to be done to fine tune this book. Thanks also to Debbie Glencross for her advice on the depiction of the chemical compounds and elements portrayed at each chapter heading; to Hamish Whyte for his continuing support and advice; to Ali Veitch and Graham

Walker, who put me right on aspects of Orkney culture; and to Tom Marshall for his counsel on court procedure and etiquette. Thanks to Kerry Houston for her invaluable assistance with cover design. As always, special thanks to Shirley, my first approach in all matters of writing and everything else. Any errors that remain are my own.

The map at the beginning is an extract from the original Air Ministry Record Site Plan of 1946, which can be seen at the Heritage Centre, Sanday. The cover depicts an early CRT radar picture. All other illustrations are copyright of the author.

The Author

Francis J Glynn lives in Aberdour with his wife, Shirley. They have visited Orkney many times with their two daughters and their families, and continue to enjoy the land, the history, the people and their hospitality.

.

28803551R00123

Printed in Great Britain
by Amazon